T0121349

Babingo
the Noble Rebel

Originally published in French as
Babingo au nom des acculturés

A NOVEL

Moussibahou Mazou

SUB-SAHARAN
PUBLISHERS

First published in Ghana 2021 by
Sub-Saharan Publishers,
P.O.Box 358,
Legon-Accra,
Ghana.

Email: saharanp@africaonline.com.gh
         akoss_oforimensah@yahoo.com

Website: www.subsaharanpublishers.com

Text and © of this English edition:
Moussibahou Mazou.

Translated from French into English by Prof.
Augustine Asaah, French Department, University
of Ghana, Legon.

ISBN: 978-9988-550-87-5

Design and typesetting by Kwabena Agyepong.

Text and © of the original French edition; Les
Éditions du Flamboyant et Communications 2018.

Copyright Notice

"If you renounce your spirituality in favour of that of your aggressor, you will forever become his slave."

A popular Asian adage

Chapter One

Alex Babingo was an exceptionally gifted and pleasant boy who was the pride of his parents, more specifically his father, Paul Makouta. Papa Makouta saw in his son the first doctor to be produced by the family, and certainly not one destined for law given that the legal profession was made for the timid, conditioned to become over time base prattlers. He might even have seen in him the future Minister of Education, and why not, the president of his dear envisioned Republic of Congo, when in the not too distant future, the people of this colony would become the masters of their own destiny.

In the manner of most of his contemporaries, Makouta projected onto his son his own ambitions, particularly those he had been unable to achieve himself. He believed that in educating his children according to European mode of expression and thought, he was giving them the rare opportunity of living as Whitemen, or better still, of appropriating their culture, the better to snatch power from them. Little did he know that by such alienation and his potentially unconscious rejection of his own culture, he was falling into a snare from which future generations would find it difficult to escape.

Papa Makouta, an administrative clerk by profession, was employed by the colonial administration around 1940 with a school certificate as his only academic credential. During this period, this priceless parchment, or even the ordinary middle school leaving certificate, was for natives the key that magically opened the door to employment in the public service. And that was no small thing.

Makouta was one of the "civilized" Westernized natives, *les* évolués[1], according to the label that the French colonialists gave to a select group of their subjects. He worked in the Department of Finance in Pointe-Noire which, the youth of the time had fancifully christened Pontoon-on-the Sea, capital of Middle Congo.

One could only climb to the rank of a "civilized native" by virtue of one's membership of the group of workers that enjoyed specific privileges. Consciously or unconsciously, these "civilized natives" offered themselves as the perfect candidates for confinement into a cultural ghetto.

---

1 During the colonial era, the term was used by the French for the small group of assimilated, Frenchified, and elitist natives, set apart from the majority of their colonized subjects in Africa, Asia, and the Caribbean. The Belgians also used the same term for the handful of colonized but westernized Africans in their colonies, i. e. the Belgian Congo, Rwanda, and Burundi. Generally, French colonial rule and that of the Belgians were harsher than British colonialism. The term "évolué" is still used in French for someone who has imbibed Western civilization. "Ils ont beaucoup évolué" means "They have become more civilized or broadminded." Translator's note: All the subsequent explanations in footnotes are by the Translator.

Invariably, the "civilized native" found himself in an ambivalent situation, wavering as he did between zealous collaboration and fiery opposition. He was torn between the pride of being a privileged subject and the pain intimately felt at his self-awareness as much as of his effective relegation to the rank of under-remunerated underling as of his status as pawn in the hands of the colonial master whom he, nonetheless, sought to completely imitate.

Makouta was therefore a "civilized native," proud of communicating daily and exclusively in French with members of his household: Madeleine Mamakouta, his official spouse, Alex Babingo, his only son, as well as Néré and Binta, the other children of his family.

Woe betide any member of the house who dared speak any of the numerous local languages. Again, under no circumstance would Makouta permit any member of his family to speak metropolitan French with what he called a Bantu accent. And whoever was overheard speaking *Kituba* with the servants was liable to a severe rebuke. Often, the culprit was compelled to undergo the torture of standing in the corner. The culprit was made to stand up, at the end of the dining room while the other members of the family enjoyed their breakfast or lunch. This was also a starvation torture.

Makouta reluctantly allowed his wife to communicate in the local language every now and then when she had to give instructions to the domestic staff, especially since he was convinced that any chance of hearing Madeleine Mamakouta speak French without accent was lost years ago.

Besides, in Makouta's household, one rarely spoke to servants. Once at table, if it so happened that he needed to ask a cook or a houseboy to bring him a forgotten spoon, he would just press a hand-bell with a shrill sound for the servant in question to show up in less than no time.

The master of the house had equally installed a bell, which he pressed at will, on the terrace located at the main gate of the residence. But Makouta sometimes broke his own rules. He spoke *Téké*, his mother tongue, when he was angry with his wife or when he wanted to communicate a secret message to Mamakouta and had no intention of letting the children in on it. Mamakouta, a nurse, was far from being in support of the regulations imposed by her husband.

Therefore, she sometimes dared to have a discussion on the matter with Makouta. She was, however, under no illusion that the discussion could degenerate into a squabble, elicit from him a blunt refusal, or simply portray them as a couple on different wavelengths, always at cross-purposes.

"My dear Papa Paul, the regulations you've instituted forbidding our children from speaking any local language at home aren't right. First of all, in my opinion, the children will lose touch with their roots if they can't express their innermost feelings in what we know to be their mother tongue. Don't forget that the overwhelming majority of our people didn't go to school and so can't express themselves in French. How do you want our children to communicate with the people around them later?"

"You can't convince me with this argument. For, if our children want to belong to the future ruling elite of this country, they must not waste their time learning to master a mode of communication which in actual fact is only a dialect. Beyond the confines of their small community, what you pompously call a language would be of no value to them. The more they master the language of power which currently controls the destiny of our country, the better they will feel at ease in this environment. Again, let me repeat, I don't want them jabbering in French with a strong Bantu accent. I don't in any way intend to change my decision. This is a decision that I would least want to go back to. So, if you don't want to incur my wrath, avoid bringing up the issue for discussion in front of the children."

One could all but picture engraved on the wooden front door of Makouta's bungalow, the inscription: *"Here, it is forbidden to speak any language apart from French."*

Like most of his colleagues, Makouta was an ardent Catholic. He was even a little more than a conventional Catholic as he was considered in the eyes of all, to be a Holy Joe. All his children were baptized. They had received the Holy Communion and the older children had even been confirmed. None could afford to be left out of Sunday mass which everybody attended, adorned in their most beautiful apparel. It was simply necessary to be in one's Sunday best, in order to appear as a model of decorum before the Lord.

That did not prevent Makouta from consulting the oracles or sounding out the will of the ancestors any time he needed to make an important decision for himself or for his family. At the drop of a hat, he would travel miles to visit the soothsayer of his village. Before writing the examination that would ensure his transition from an auxiliary agent to a public servant, the great diviner gave him a potion with which he had to rub all over his body every morning for thirty days before the D-day.

Not for once did he leave behind the amulet which uncle Ngasono had offered him when he was about to leave his native village near Lekana to assume his new post in Pointe-Noire. Mamakouka, his wife, and all their children had their skins covered with small scars. These were scarifications, more or less old, resulting from the ravages of protective powders applied, in the past, against the evil eye.

Makouta and his contemporaries could simultaneously be Christians, Muslims, and followers of African ancestral worship. The

Muslim who regularly consulted his *mallam*[2] also had his arms distinctively laden with *juju* charms.

Such was the "civilized native" with his ambivalence. Such was Makouta. French therefore became the mother tongue of the family, on the intransigent order of the paterfamilias. This unconscious acculturation vis-à-vis the French language did not prevent Paul Makouta from being a fierce and active pro-independence militant.

The Overseas Reform Act[3], introduced some ten years after the end of the Second World War, according to which indigenes of the colonies could from then on enjoy a certain autonomy without having to leave the Republic of France, no longer met the aspirations of the

----

2   Although *mallam* or *malam* originally means "teacher" in Arabic "mu'allim", in Anglophone Africa he has often assumed the additional functions of a healer, a soothsayer, and a spiritual protector, almost as his counterpart in Francophone Africa, the *marabout*, has.

3   *La Loi-cadre Gaston Defferre,* commonly known as *La Loi-cadre*, passed on June 23, 1956 by the French National Assembly.

administrative clerk and his fellow militants of the "Independence Now!" movement.

The Makouta family lived in the cozy neighbourhood of Pointe-Noire, a place reserved for "civilized natives," those who dressed in suits made of well-starched percale and a colonial helmet made of cork, everything in a strikingly immaculate whiteness. The "civilized native" civil servants made superhuman efforts to resemble their metropolitan colleagues, as were then called the colonial civil servants who came from France. The "civilized native" did not just want to resemble the White man, he equally considered it his legitimate right to take over the latter's place, at the opportune time, and this, the earlier the better.

Freshly appointed "metropolitan civil servant" after the reform of the colonial system aimed at giving an illusion of assimilation to the natives, Makouta burned with impatience to spend his vacation in Metropolitan France which would, as a matter of time, administratively become his country of origin once he had acquired the necessary length of service in the category of "metropolitan civil servant." Upon return from vacation in Metropolitan France, he would be transferred to another French territory or even within his own country of origin, as an expatriate civil servant belonging to the famous Civil Service corps of Overseas France. Paradoxically, Makouta would then become an expatriate in his own country. But while awaiting the realization of this happy turn of events, he dreamt of sending his son, Alex Babingo, to Metropolitan France to continue his studies.

When young Alex Babingo was enrolled in school at age five, most of his classmates were two or three years older than him. Alex Babingo could already read, write some simple words and count the numbers from one to hundred in French. This was a feat for a boy of his age. In his first year at the primary school, he was among the few pupils capable of understanding the words pronounced by the instructor to teach them the rudiments of the French language. Babingo was one of the few children who spoke French at home. He could even boast of having just skipped through classes during his pre-nursery school years.

It was not uncommon for Alex Babingo to correct the teacher when the latter committed errors during French or arithmetic exercises. This sometimes made him get punished for boisterousness. At the primary school certificate examination, Alex Babingo emerged as one of the first ten successful pupils out of the one thousand candidates that passed in the whole territory.

A good-looking chap, Babingo was the darling of the girls of a school situated not far away from his.

Chapter Two

As pupils from the same neighbourhood, Alex and Tessa developed the habit of walking some distance together on the way to their respective schools. While on the way, Tessa frequently chanced upon some of her parents' friends. Naturally, she lost no time in always greeting them in *Kituba*, the language used by the majority of the inhabitants of Pointe-Noire to communicate among themselves

Tessa handled *Kituba* with an ease that impressed Alex. Full of admiration but puzzled, he asked Tessa why her parents had not banned her from using the local language. Surprised, the young girl at first did not know how to answer. She kept silent, especially because she feared offending her school friend. Babingo was, as said earlier, a cute boy, precocious and very sharp for his age. Quite visible on the left side of his perfectly brushed hair, was a nice parting which gave him the looks of a boy just coming from the Gold Coast. When he smiled, the dimples on his two cheeks highlighted an irresistible charm.

At ten years old, he was often gripped by an emotion rather premature for his age at the simple sight of Tessa, his favourite friend. It must be admitted that the schoolgirl, slightly older than him, did not go unnoticed because of her astounding beauty. With an hourglass body shape, bright and bewitching eyes, Tessa had on her long neck, the head of a resurrected Nefertiti. Of a particularly shining blackness, her extraordinarily long hair reached the lowest part of her back. Tessa finally resolved to answer a question she initially pretended not to understand.

Even though the young lad had internalized Makouta's directive of expressing himself exclusively in the French language no matter who the interlocutor was, the young girl succeeded in convincing him of the absurdity of this order. She proceeded with the condemnation of Makouta's directive in the nicest way possible. However, before that, it was Babingo who had challenged her.

"Why don't your parents forbid you from speaking *Kituba*?," he insisted.

"Alex, be clear with your question; I don't understand you", she replied.

"In our house, my parents, or rather my father prohibits us from speaking any other language apart from French. He does not want us to show any Bantu accent when speaking French. He also says that if we do not get used to expressing ourselves in French at home, we will have problems understanding our lessons in school. Dad's order is strict. At home, whoever dares speak *Téké*, the language spoken in the village, or *Kituba* the common language of the domestic staff is severely punished. Everybody must obey this order."

"I think your father's order is difficult to understand. The majority of the inhabitants here in the city only speak *Kituba*. Apart from this language and three or four other languages of the country, my mother cannot speak any foreign language; she does not understand French. Besides, whether she speaks French or not, that has no importance since here in our city, everybody speaks *Kituba*. If you want to be understood by the majority of the people, you must at least learn to express yourself in *Kituba*."

"I understand, but how would I dare defy my father's directive without giving myself away? Indeed, I want to start learning to speak *Kituba* with you, but how do I avoid making the mistake of speaking it to the servants once at home?"

"Listen, it's simple. You choose only one person outside of your home with whom you will speak *Kìtuba*. It is said that children can change from one language to the other effortlessly. It's therefore possible to speak *Kìtuba* if you wish to without you being found out by your father. I really want to train you to speak *Kìtuba*. If you agree, we'll only speak it when we're alone on our way between school and home."

The two teenagers therefore decided to speak only *Kìtuba* between them every morning on their way to school, thus defying Papa Makouta's order. Alex Babingo resorted to a lot of tricks to avoid making the mistake of speaking a prohibited language at home. While the servants thought that they were hiding their little games from him by using *Kìtuba* among themselves, Babingo knew what was being plotted, but restrained himself from reacting.

Months went by and no one detected any Bantu accent in Alex Babingo's spoken French. Meanwhile, he was already mastering *Kìtuba* to the point of even adorning it with the proverbs learnt from Tessa's school who herself had leant from her grandmother the art of embellishing speech with proverbs. The two young friends jealously kept their secret until the day when Babingo was to embark on an overseas journey, alas far, very far away from Pointe-Noire, and most especially from Tessa, his friend.

Chapter Three

Buoyed by the scholarly feats of his son, Paul Makouta decided to send Alex Babingo to Metropolitan France to commence his secondary school education. By the end of summer which coincided with the rainy season in his country, Makouta had got ready the outfit of the future traveler: a pullover made of thick wool bought from the boutique of a Portuguese merchant in town, shoes lined with fur inside, a hat, shirts made of cotton and all the paraphernalia of a complete traveler soon to confront for the first time snow and the other rigors of winter.

At that time, enrolment into a French school was child's play, and still much easier if one was moving administratively from one French territory to the other. Besides, the identity card which served as Alex Babingo's travel document bore, in bold characters, the word *French* in the column for holder's "nationality."

It was under a pelting rain, at the end of the morning of a day in September in the year 1952 that Alex Babingo accompanied by Makouta his father, Mamakouta his mother and two other friends of his, arrived at the Pointe-Noire train station. Also there to wish Alex safe journey were some other family members as well as his male and female friends among whom was Tessa. The young traveler was leaving for Brazzaville from where he would continue his trip by air.

The daily connection between the two towns was done frequently via the railway line called *Congo-Ocean Railway*, plied by locomotives which the natives wrongly referred to as "high speed train". Almost five hundred and ten kilometers in length, the *Congo-Ocean Railway* which linked and still links till today the capital of Middle Congo to Brazzaville was a grandiose and monumental work whose economic and social value is incontestable. But this railway line, rightly described as *bloody works*, was constructed by the colonial administration under the mercilessly rigorous scheme of hard labour to which the natives were subjected. Tens of thousands of natives died from accidents as a result of frequent cave-ins, diseases, and maltreatment.

At that time, the colonizer arrogantly did not care to know about the international convention against hard labour. It was at the high cost of the sacrifice made by the workers, most often deportees, that the journey from Pointe-Noire to Brazzaville which Babingo was about to undertake, was going to last for some hours instead of several days had it been undertaken earlier using the unwelcoming tracks when this railway line was only a dense forest.

When Babingo and those accompanying him arrived at the station, the train which

would take Babingo from Pointe-Noire to Brazzaville was already in. If all went as planned,
he would reach his destination late in the afternoon. While other passengers were bustling
around them, Makouta continued to advise
Alex Babingo profusely. However, the boy's
attention was rather riveted on Tessa, the friend
he would have to leave behind.

For her part, Tessa stole a glance at Babingo,
rather hurriedly, so as not to attract the attention
of the elderly people present. The first whistle
of the station master signaled the impending
departure of the train. Everybody was moving
on the platform. Travelers and those accompanying them waved brightly coloured scarves,
while lifting their arms to say goodbye to family
members and friends they would soon leave.

Alex Babingo was one of the last travelers
to board the train. At the very moment that
he was going to give his last goodbye hugs to
his parents, Tessa removed a necklace made of
cowry from her neck which she swiftly sneaked

into the right side pocket of Babingo's jacket. She shouted "bye" and pronounced some sentences in impeccable *Kituba*. Alex Babingo responded likewise with a little hesitation, to the great astonishment of his parents.

After a deafening whistle, the train started its journey, slowly leaving the platform and well-wishers. Makouta, his spouse, Tessa, and others followed the train with their eyes until Babingo's friendly arm disappeared into the horizon.

The young boy was embarking upon his first outing from his birthplace to discover villages, which to him were all strange, as the train stopped at a countless number of stations. There was "the *Saras*" station, so named in memory of the workmen deported from Chad to take part in the construction of the railway. These workers who came from far away paid a heavy price in this enterprise. The *Bandas*, another station, evoked the memory of the rail workers from Ubangi-Shari[4]. They were also enrolled by force and had to pay dearly with their lives and their toil in this nightmare that the construction site of *Congo-Ocean Railway* became.

The stop at Dolisie reminded Alex Babingo about what he had learnt about this French explorer, Savorgnan de Brazza's companion to whom the latter entrusted Loango and the opening of the Niari-Kwilu road. The history of Dolisie railway station is synonymous with that of the town with the same name, founded in 1934 after the inauguration of the railway.

At each train stop, Alex Babingo observed with amusement the sight and sounds offered by fruits and vegetable sellers together with traders of dried or smoked meat, cassava, sweets and drinks of different flavours. One could never imagine a more colourful crowd of traders of different ages, all attempting to offer

---

4   The French colony then known as Ubangi-Shari (Oubangui-Chari in French) derived its name from the two rivers, Ubangi and Shari. In 1958, two years before independence, Ubangi-Shari adopted the name, Central African Republic.

their wares at the most enticing prices to travelers some of whom appeared indifferent.

On the contrary, other passengers, more familiar with the prices of consumer goods in Brazzaville, took advantage of the golden opportunity to shop. After eight hours, the *Micheline* arrived finally at the Brazzaville railway terminus, where Babingo's aunt, Mafouta was waiting on the steps, surrounded by her two daughters, Kissassi and Massissi. They were delighted to meet their cousin. As custom demanded, they would not just welcome Alex Babingo to their home, but would feel obliged to show him the major historical attractions of Brazzaville which the boy had so much heard about at school but had never seen. Saint Anne Basilica of Congo, Félix Eboué Stadium, General De Gaulle's statue and many other places that were equally famous.

His cousins will also show him *Poto-Poto*.

And there it was! *Poto-Poto*, this neighborhood located at the heart of the sprawling city was very well-known for its cosmopolitism, and famed across the world for the meeting place it uniquely offered to merrymakers, thanks to the legendary dancing bar called "Chez Faignon."

But first of all, they needed to reach Aunt Mafouta's home. The over-crowded bus in which Aunt Mafouta, Babingo, and his cousins were crammed from the station stopped every five minutes for passengers who were apparently not in a hurry to alight or board. The snail pace of the bus was going to jeopardize the plans of the young ones.

Finally Aunt Mafouta's stylishly cute house –a legacy from her late husband – situated on Mafoundou Road, welcomed the young Alex who saw himself offered the traditional welcoming water before the sampling of dishes prepared in his honour. Alex Babingo just had the time to eat some pieces of cassava, *saka saka*, in the accompaniment of chicken and *mouembe* lovingly cooked by his aunt. For her, it was out of the question for her nephew to take the plane on an empty stomach. The visits to different sites in Brazzaville were undertaken at the double. They needed to be fast about it as the young traveler had to use a public bus in order to arrive on time at the agency of the airline company, charged with conveying passengers to the airport.

Kassissi, the older of the cousins, volunteered to accompany Alex Babingo downtown. Massissi, the younger, who did not want to be left out, protested vehemently and succeeded in convincing her sister and Babingo that she should also join the party. Alex Babingo had already observed that since his arrival, his cousins had never ceased outdoing each other in demonstrations of kindness towards him. The over-attentiveness of his cousins was neither feigned nor completely disinterested. It was a matter of who would be more appreciated by the charming boy leaving for studies in *mpoutou*. Each of the two sisters wanted to position herself to be the chosen one.

But Babingo had neither the mind nor the inclination to give in to sentiments. Therefore, it was with conventional hugs and kisses that Alex Babingo parted company with his cousins before leaving in a special bus for the airport.

In the bus that was ready to head for the airport around six o'clock in the evening, there were about twenty people; men, women, and children dressed in their Sunday best, the largest in number being expatriates returning to Metropolitan France for good or going there for vacation. At this time, the roads had been invaded by cyclists returning from work and they spilled like a swarm over the roads in Poto-Poto and other neighborhoods. The driver of the bus had to apply a thousand and one tricks especially the use of his horn, to avoid hitting certain careless cyclists.

At last the airport! The main lobby of Maya Maya was milling with people. One could easily differentiate travelers and those accompanying them from the mere onlookers. Some were standing in front of the main entrance, dreamily, while those who had specific reasons to be there bustled frantically.Not far from the departure counter, a hostess held behind the ticket office a microphone from which she was busy sending out probably an important piece of information. However, this announcement was rendered extremely inaudible because uttered in a nasal voice.

However, thanks to the movements of the queuing crowd one could guess that the passengers were finally being invited to the departure gate. Some were dressed to confront the anticipated cold in the plane and in France, others held their coat on their arm while the most foolhardy among them had put on light clothing as if they were going to a seaside station in the tropics. An overexcited Alex Babingo tried in vain to identify a familiar face in the crowd of passengers. In turns and with reverent silence, the passengers boarded the aircraft after showing their boarding passes to a couple of agents dressed in the distinctive uniform of the sole airline company.

The caravel which was transporting Alex Babingo and his fellow travelers to Paris gave one the impression of being jam-packed. The comings and goings of the cabin crew aggravated the inevitable agitation provoked by such a concentration of people in such a small space. Ahead of him in the first row of the cabin, Alex Babingo noticed two teenagers, who, like him, were probably going to France for their studies. Somehow intimidated, he could not get up to enquire from them about their final destination. He would probably have the opportunity to do so on arrival.

All of a sudden, a man with a grey-flowing beard and who was wearing a white cassock underneath a grey corduroy jacket, came to sit by the young traveler. *Tomorrow, we will be in Paris or in Heaven*, remarked the "moundélé" priest, half mockingly, half apprehensively. This gloomy outburst from the religious man was not to the liking of the adolescent for whom Paris was certainly synonymous with paradise, but a paradise on earth. The clergyman, who had guessed the motive of the adolescent's journey, engaged him in a conversation.

"My son, I bet you're going to France to pursue your studies, unless of course you're going there to join your parents."

"Father, you're right, my parents are sending me to Metropolitan France first, for my secondary school education and later, the university."

"In which French region will you be? I hope your parents have gotten you an institution located in a region with a bearable climate, where winter isn't too severe."

"I've been registered in a college at Bagnères-de-Bigorre. But I don't know if winter there is inclement or not."

"Bagnères-de-Bigorre is a small town in the south-west founded as far back as the century before our time. Its rather cool climate, whatever the season, is milder than that of the central and northern parts of France. You'll be fine there, my son."

And, without even worrying about the denomination to which the adolescent belonged, he spoke to him at length about the church which he could attend. While the clergyman, like a historical bard, was waxing lyrical on the qualities of a church built in the Gothic style of the 14th century, Babingo had sunk into the arms of Morpheus. From time to time, he tried to pull a cover cloth over his head to protect himself from the freezing cold coming from the air-conditioning system of the aircraft.

With an instinctive gesture and as if lost in a dream, he dipped his right hand into his pocket to cling tightly to the cowry necklace which Tessa had slipped there when he was leaving Pointe-Noire. The aircraft flew for hours while Alex Babingo slept deeply. Suddenly, the flight crew turned the light on, probably to draw attention to the next landing of the aircraft at a transit airport. This light as well as the movements up and down woke Babingo up and the other passengers who clearly were finding it difficult shaking off their drowsiness.

The cabin manager reassured the passengers by announcing to them that the touchdown at Tripoli was scheduled for one hour thirty minutes, and that after this stop, they were going to be served breakfast and hot drinks. Little comfort, Babingo observed, for the minutes of sleep of which he had been robbed.

A simple airbase during the Italian domination, Tripoli became an international airport when the Royal Air Force was established there in the beginning of the 1940s. At that time, airplanes travelled the distance between Brazzaville and Paris in about thirty-six hours.

The caravel landed at an airport which looked like a military airbase. The stocking up on fuel took about an hour. Thereafter, the aircraft took off again, cleft through the sky and was lost in the clouds for hours on end from the perspective of the young traveler who could no longer fall asleep. Above the clouds, the sky was strikingly blue.

The clergyman seemed to be enjoying this moment and it was with gusto that he devoured the buttered bread, marmalade, ham omelet, fruits, and other delicacies that covered the tray which the air hostess had presented him with a conventional smile. Not far from Babingo's seat, other passengers apparently more tired, continued sleeping thus adding their snoring to the prevailing noise.

This atmosphere had the knack for creating in Alex Babingo, a feeling of anxiety mixed with fantasy. The anxiety stemming from the sheer distance of a journey he was undertaking for the first time; and the fantasy that surrounded the discovery of the capital of Metropolitan France, Paris, of which he had heard so much.

It was under a hazy and menacing afternoon sky that the Orly airport welcomed the passengers. They all seemed to miss the damp heat of Brazzaville which they had left, hardly a day earlier. It was, however, in a happy mood tinged with anxiety, that they congratulated one another and thanked God to have brought them safe and sound, to their destination.

Downstairs, not far from the gangway, two shuttle buses were waiting for them, with the engine in motion. After bringing on board all the passengers who were almost unrecognizable in their thick coats, the buses dropped them off in a vast room where immigration service officers were waiting for them behind their counters. Mere formalities which were done with quickly, because at that time, people arriving from the French community had no need for a visa to enter France, since they were, either metropolitans or nationals from an overseas French territory.

Outside the airport, other buses waiting for passengers moved towards the center of the capital city where they alighted in front of the airline's headquarters. On arrival at the terminal, Babingo had just enough time to exchange

a few words with the other young passengers,
lucky holders of French Community scholarship, being treated to an official reception,
unlike him.

He was, however, welcomed by his father's
friend, Galin Doite. Makouta and Galin Doite
first met in Pointe-Noire when all the administrative offices were housed in the magnificent
building called the Audinot Tower constructed
in the form of a horse-shoe. They were also
friends in the same posh neighborhood. At
the end of the week, they often found themselves playing bowls, French style, with other
colleagues.

A court clerk by trade, by dint of determination and sacrifices, Galin Doite took some
courses by correspondence and succeeded
in obtaining an Advanced Level Certificate
in Law. Admitted to pursue further studies in
Paris, Galin Doite brilliantly landed his first
degree in Law. He fought to enter the École

nationale de la France d'outre-mer (Overseas National School of France).

Once a mere training center at its establishment in 1885 to provide training for about ten officers of Khmer origin, the Cambodian School was quickly transformed into a "Colonial School," open to numerous metropolitans who chose to work in the overseas public service. The colonial school was mandated to train "the leaders of the Empire" in diverse areas of specialization. It was to render more visible the presence of the Republic in all the nooks and crannies of French colonies. Administrators, governors, and governor-generals were conditioned to apply and assert the imperial doctrine of France in the performance of their functions.

Later, probably in response to emergent imperatives, the Colonial School, which had already been rechristened the National School of Overseas France, opened its doors to the French middle class, beneficiaries of the free education it offered. Again, many years later, in consequence of the principle of Africanization of officers of overseas administration introduced by the Reform Act of 1956, the School welcomed a large number of sub-Saharan Africans and Madagascans.

ENFOM (L'École Nationale de la France d'Outre-Mer) which became the Institute of Overseas Higher Studies (IHEOM), and later the International Institute of Public Administration, was the breeding ground for the first batch of senior civil servants and politicians from whose ranks emerged some of the most prominent figures in independent Francophone Africa.

Galin Doite belonged to the last cohort of ENFOM graduates.

Chapter Four

. . . .

Uncle Galin Doite considered it his duty to take Alex Babingo under his wings. Once at the train station, they took the subway, the fastest and the least expensive means of transportation for moving about in the capital. Galin Doite took advantage of the lapse that this journey provided him to teach Alex the practical geography of how to use public transport in general, especially the Parisian subway. The time they spent at the station cafeteria for a meal was also suitable for the usual pieces of advice on how to conduct oneself in all circumstances.

"Alex, you know you aren't on scholarship. Your parents or to be more specific your father is making a huge sacrifice by sending you to a private secondary school here in France. To pay back his trust and the great ambition that your father harbours for you, you must be devoted to your studies and avoid bad company."

As a good and well-trained child, Alex Babingo acquiesced to each word of wise counsel that came from Uncle Galin Doite. But while he was crunching the slices of chips and the big chicken thigh which his uncle had ordered for him, he could not take his eyes off the itinerary card that Papa Makouta had given him for the rest of his journey.

And when Uncle Galin Doite informed him that he could accompany Alex Babingo to Bagnères-de-Bigorre, it was with a big smile that the teenager demonstrated his immense joy. The young traveler was very much eager to visit Paris. Like all children of his age, the City of Light made him fantasize so much. But there was no time for dreams. As the tickets for the two of them had already been procured by

Galin Doite for the Paris-Bagnères-de-Bigorre journey, it was now time to follow Uncle, find the coach and above all, the couchettes which had been allocated to them.

Babingo did not realize that he was going to undertake another long trip before arriving at his future home base. But for now, he and Uncle Galin Doite had to look for and sit in the coach whose number featured on their tickets. Two rows of double bunks were waiting for them. As they were the first to find themselves in the coach, Uncle Galin Doite asked the conductor if he could choose two among the four couchettes.

"You are lucky, the officer responded. You will be the only passengers in this compartment up to the terminus."

Their choice naturally was the two couchettes at the top where they could settle themselves in all security, with their personal effects. At dusk, they quickly understood they had to resign themselves to the fact they would not be able to admire the landscapes that the train would pass through during its journey. They, however, consoled themselves that each of them could have a couchette big enough to endure this long journey.

Some minutes before 11 pm, the station master gave the departure signal for the train which first set off slowly then ran at the speed of a railcar toward the faraway destination, sited in the southern part of the country. At night, during the stopover at the big stations, the abrupt braking of the locomotive would wake passengers up from their half-sleep even as they were struggling to decipher the names of the towns they had crossed by looking out through the window.

Early in the morning, the train finally arrived at Toulouse, its terminus. With reddened eyes, signs of a night sleep interrupted many times, Uncle Galin Doite and Babingo disembarked from the coach, relieved.

Very conveniently, Magloire was on the platform carrying a small placard with the name of "Alex Babingo, the boarder," written on it. Magloire was one of the boarding house supervisors at Sacred Heart Junior High School (Collège du Sacré-Cœur) who was responsible for welcoming new boarders.

After brief introductions and some words of welcome, during which Galin Doite introduced himself, Magloire helped his guests to place their baggage in the car booth of an old 2CV Citroen vehicle, the sole and indispensable liaison vehicle of the school. Everything appeared strange to the young traveler who was listening attentively to the story of Bagnères-de-Bigorre being narrated by the supervisor.

After some hours of drive on hilly roads, the driver of the 2CV stopped sharply before the main gate to the school. The principal of the school, Mr. David Dupont, informed about the arrival of the young African and the accompanying person, stepped out of his office to welcome them.

The usual words of welcome over, Babingo and his uncle were in the hands of the main supervisor who took them first to a room which served as the cafeteria where they were served with coffee and hot cocoa drink. After giving his Paris contacts to the main supervisor, Galin Doite took his leave of both of them, muttering some words to signify that he was ready to assume the functions of a guardian for the young boarder.

The guide showed Alex Babingo his dormitory and other places which would thenceforth be his common living space with other boys. The discovery of life in a boarding house caused a shock in this teenager who up till then had never lived outside his family residence in the cozy neighbourhood of Pointe-Noire. His room-mates were naturally curious to know the reasons for the presence, amongst them, of a boy from a very distant country. One of them tried asking this strange question:

"What have you done to make your parents send you to a boarding house right from Form One in a country so far away from yours?"

Unaware of the reasons for such an unexpected question, Alex Babingo did not know how to respond to it. In fact, he did not know that some of the boarders had a past replete with sad stories for children of their age. Most of them had divorced or separated parents. Others were there because their parents were in foreign countries, for professional reasons. For a good number of these young ones, the boarding house was a haven.

In this world of children from so many peculiar backgrounds, Alex Babingo stood at once by his balanced behaviour, his seriousness at work, and his remarkable urbanity. His rich vocabulary surprised his teachers. As a consequence, he was quickly appointed the class representative. Alex Babingo became friends with

Philippe, one of his roommates. Philippe was one of the so-called Public Welfare[5] children. The protection of vulnerable persons featured among the numerous assignments of an organization created for that purpose.

As a fatherless and motherless orphan, Philip had been entrusted to the care of the brothers of a Catholic congregation at Bagnères-de-Bigorre who put him in the boarding house. When the school was closed at the end of the week, he was housed in one of the guest houses of this religious society.

Lonely and lacking family relations, Philip threw himself body and soul into substance abuse which ruined his health and ended up compromising his future. The favourite occupation of this boy was pouring drying glue in a plastic bag. He would then place the mouth of the container on his mouth and nose to inhale the vapour. The poor boy always had need for more tubes of glue to satisfy his desire. He

---

5   Also called National Assistance Board.

was so much dependent on it that it ended up damaging his respiratory organ and his eyeball. Whenever he could afford it financially, he "stoned himself" by taking a harder drug.

Alex Babingo bonded with this boy whose tragic story he eventually got to know. And it was with compassion and especially, the passion which a boy of his age muster, that he defended Philip, each time the school administration threatened to dismiss his friend.

Alas! Philip was going through an irremediable descent into hell. Babingo, the class representative and his friend, could do nothing when the college's disciplinary committee proposed to the principal to expel Philip from the school before the end of the school year.

Alex Babingo played basketball in the team coached by the school's physical education and sports teacher. He very well liked practicing this sport in which he could show genuine dexterity. Frequent competitions with the students from other schools of the region gave him the opportunity to meet pleasant people and have vital socialization. Babingo was conscious of his charisma around other students. It was a matter of who wanted to be the best friend of the African. He was also a member of a choir in town. This group of people from different backgrounds loved to come together regularly at the school's big sports centre where they spent very nice time together. Benefitting from a precociously developed mature baritone voice, Babingo soon wormed himself into the heart of all.

One day, during a funeral ceremony for a member of the group, the choristers were invited, in turns, to sing, preferably in their mother tongue. Cameroonian, Vietnamese, Madagascan, Congolese, and of course French. Each chorister was to render a religiously-inspired song in the form of prayer to the memory of the deceased.

It was total panic when it was Babingo's turn. It was impossible for him to offer a song in his mother tongue. The rudiments of *Kituba* which Tessa had taught him were of no help to enable him write and even less, to improvise a refrain in this language. Incredulous, the other choristers thought their baritone singer was bluffing them. Or worse, that he hated his own mother tongue. He sincerely objected to this, but no one believed him.

Engulfed in shame, Babingo realized the sheer depth of his deracination. But how would he able to free himself of such humiliating disappointments? He contemplated calling Tessa to narrate his misfortune at first hand to her. Unfortunately at that time, the telephone was a means of communication out of the common man's reach. The invention of cellular telephone was probably still at the stage of fiction in the head of its creator. Babingo then resolved to write to Tessa, the very first missive to her since his departure.

"*My dear Tessa,*

Since my departure from home, it is the first time that I'm writing to you. I'm ashamed of my conduct but please, don't take my silence for lack of respect towards you.

I've very little time at my disposal because my life as a student here is full of unforeseen events and the pace of work leaves me with little time to do other things beyond my studies.

In the boarding school, the hours for lessons, meals, and sleeping are regulated to the minute.

Weekends are reserved for attending church in the company of the guardian in charge of my catechesis and members of his family. They're very devout and there's no question of me missing Sunday mass. At times, we even have to go to the stadium to watch football matches. I must admit that these are moments I impatiently wait for, most importantly when my favourite team is playing.

I'm also a member of the choir managed by one of my school teachers. We train every Monday evening with others living outside the school. Our practice takes place just after dinner to end an hour later, because of the firm instruction of the overall supervisor as regards sleeping hours. We make ourselves available when we're asked to perform. In this regard, I've just gone through a distressing experience.

At the funeral of a former member of the choir, each of us was asked to say a prayer or sing a religious song in our mother tongue. I couldn't do it for as you know my knowledge of Kituba and even of Téké, was still very basic when I was leaving the country. My mates interpreted my refusal as a lack of respect for them.

How could they understand that someone from Africa is incapable of expressing himself in another language other than French? But that was my case.

I'm locked up in a shameful silence. In effect, I'm ashamed to confess to them that my father forbade me from speaking another language but French because he didn't want me to pick up a nasty accent.

I remembered what you told me; but how could I imagine that one day, far away from my country, some people would ask me to express myself in my native language? My shame was greater than the disappointment of my fellow choristers.

I've sworn that one day, I'll wash away this shame, even if I've to choose the path of rebellion because of that."

Babingo's life went on without any incident at the Sacred Heart College, in the small and *serene* town of Bagnères-de-Bigorre. Contrary to the practice that students of his age returned to their countries for long vacations, Papa Makouta preferred sending his son to holiday camps organized by the welfare services of schools, labour unions, or scout associations.

After some years, Alex Babingo could boast of having crisscrossed the whole of France. He went from one holiday camp to the other; from the south to the center and from the east to the west of the Hexagon. He would without doubt have preferred to return to Pointe-Noire to spend his holidays with his family and see his friend, Tessa, again.

But he had to succumb to Papa Makouta's orders. Bagnères-de Bigorre school did not have a programme for the last three years of high school that could enable Alex Babingo study for the standard baccalaureate he desired to obtain. At that time, candidates had a choice between three tracks, Latin-Greek, Latin-Modern Languages or Modern languages.

In the Sixth Form[6] of Toulouse where he had to register to pursue his studies in the last three years of secondary school in the chosen track, Alex Babingo found himself in a social milieu almost similar to what he had experienced earlier. Some of his classmates came from countries located in the four corners of the world. There, he notably met Anthony whose parents were Americans. The father, an engineer, was the technical officer in an aircraft assembly factory near Toulouse. Another friend named Gerard was the son of a famous wine merchant.

With some of his Toulouse senior high school mates, Alex Babingo not only had the feeling of finding himself again in a familiar

6   *Lycée* in French; the equivalent of senior high school or senior secondary school.

context, but also of meeting people who shared his condition as a foreigner. His senior high school days also coincided with his self-discovery and sense of freedom, affirmation of his personality, and the beginning of student militancy. Organised holidays in scout camps would thenceforth become a thing of the past

In Toulouse, a university town of great repute, Alex Babingo also met compatriots most of whom were students of law, medicine, mathematics, and even agronomy. He loved visiting this group of people who were older than him and whose vast political knowledge he admired. When he succeeded in obtaining an exeat to go out of school, he liked to visit those he called his elders in a popular night club, "Le Baobab" very highly appreciated by the Africans in Toulouse and its environs. There, he learnt the trendy dances from Bongonina, known as the undisputed master of the subject. It was during these meetings that he developed the political awareness and strong multicultural awakening diametrically opposed to what Papa Makouta extolled. It was the beginning of his long journey towards what will be a soft, non-violent, and noble rebellion.

Chapter Five

During the summer holidays, Babingo liked to sit down on the terrace of the café of the popular Capitole Square called le Bibent, where he could watch tourists passing as he struggled to guess their nationalities. It was both a hobby and his special way of travelling around the world.

Le Bibent could pride itself on having been the place where Jean Jaurès, then municipal counsellor, wrote his articles for a famous newspaper called *La Dépêche*. People also say that it was on the terrace of this legendary café that three Serbian students conceived of the plan of assassinating the Austro-Hungarian Crown Prince, Archduke François Ferdinand and his wife, in Sarajevo. The act committed by these three accomplices of a pan-Slav association was the drop of water which made the vessel overflow and engendered the First World War in a Europe, already weakened by antagonistic alliances and agreements.

One scorching afternoon, Alex Babingo's gaze stopped dead on a young and pretty tourist whose traits, especially her striking blondness suggested that she came from Northern Europe. The well-known attraction of opposites seemed to have occurred. The pretty blond stared at Alex Babingo and ended up getting very close to him. Without ceremony, she asked him if she could touch his hair.

Surprised, Alex Babingo wanted to know the reasons for such a request which was as bold as it was unexpected.

"For what reason do you want to touch my hair?" he asked the blonde lady.

The young woman responded with astonishing candor that she came from a country isolated from the rest of the world where she had never had the opportunity of meeting someone like him, let alone touching him.

"Where do you come from? And what's your name?"

"I'm an Icelander and my name is Ingrid Jöndöttir. Literally, Iceland means "the land of ice", the young woman clarified. "Iceland is the biggest volcanic island of the world. In actual fact, it's a small island State of the Atlantic Ocean, located between Greenland and Norway, towards the North-East of the Faroe Islands. The sun stealthily shows up there two to three months out of twelve. I presume you come from Africa."

"Africa isn't a country but a continent. I come from one of the numerous countries of the continent. This country is called Middle Congo, a French colony. My surname is Babingo and my first name is Alex."

"Speak slowly if you want me to understand you, since my French is basic," declared Ingrid to his interlocutor whose delivery was as fast as the speed of a rocket ship.

"To be able to touch my hair, you must first make a commitment."

"And what's this commitment?"

"That of giving me a kiss on my mouth."

By means of this condition, the young man thought of putting paid to the brazen request of this stranger. But Ingrid accepted the bargain with an enthusiasm that staggered Alex Babingo and encouraged him to bid higher. He attempted convincing Ingrid to accompany him to "Le Baobab", his favorite dance hall.

Even though she agreed to give a kiss on Alex Babingo's mouth, the young woman initially rejected the offer to go to a night club, arguing that her stay in Toulouse was coming to an end the following day. She needed to return to Paris early in the morning to rejoin the group of tourists she was part of and which she had left behind for sightseeing in the Pink City.

Alex Babingo insisted, claiming that it was a short walk from the night club. Whenever she wanted, Ingrid could return to the guest house where she was lodging. A kiss as shy as it was furtive on Babingo's mouth served as Ingrid's first commitment. The appointment at "Le Baobab" having finally been accepted, Alex Babingo promised to fetch the beautiful blond girl in her hotel at the agreed time.

Alex and Ingrid made a noticeable entry into "Le Baobab". The young man went toward his friends' habitual corner, did the usual introductions, and sat his new friend down.

The evening was full of demonstrations of dances and very spirited political discussions.

That was the time when *mambo*, a dance from Cuba, had become the latest rage in the best dance halls of the city. That evening, the dance floor of "Le Baobab" saw performances, in the midst of entertaining applause, by the student and no less virtuoso dancer Bongonina who made the most frenzied demonstrations, pulling numerous lovers of music to the dance floor. Babingo and Ingrid were not outdone. But even though they seemed carried away by this electric atmosphere, Babingo soon joined the group of his elders seated around the big table, far from the dance floor. This corner of the dance hall was known to be the favorite haunt of African students.

Naturally, they discussed the living conditions of students in France. They touched on the activities of the Federation of African Students in France (FEANF) as they seized the opportunity to remind themselves about the next Congress of the famous union. However, it was neither the place nor the moment to give Alex details of the life of this famous student association. He would know much more at the right time.

Nonetheless, he was briefly introduced to the origins of this student movement which played a decisive role in the early development of an ardent pan-Africanism. The movement also played a major role in the call for the total liberation of Africa at a time when majority of African leaders considered independence as a utopia or worse, a dangerous students' slogan. Nothing else was needed to convince Babingo that this pan-African student movement was the place where he could make a case for the urgency and imperative of the teaching of national languages as a fundamental cultural issue.

Persuaded that this was the right student movement he needed to fulfil his dream, he became a full member and later, was particularly active in its academic wing in Toulouse. When Alex Babingo accompanied the young girl back to the guest house, he tried to keep her for some time so that they could continue their conversations. At first, they stood on the threshold of the front door where their seduction game continued. Next, the process of seduction having had its effect, Ingrid accepted to receive her knight of the day in her room.

They talked about Middle Congo, Babingo's country; they talked about Reykjavik, Ingrid's hometown; they talked about the beauty of the fjords in Iceland, they talked about Ingrid's job. They talked about the spellbinding, teeming, and iconic African neighborhood of Pointe-Noire. They had some cups of coffee to prolong the conversation which soon assumed the character of effusions. And, almost without realizing it, Ingrid and Alex gave themselves up to each other. And what should happen between a man and a woman happened.

Having barely finished their lovemaking, the two lovebirds were thrown into a long silence as if, suddenly, the profound incongruity of their amorous fury had just dawned upon them. They pulled apart from each other late in the night for the senior high school student had to return to his hall of residence before daybreak. They promised to maintain their relationship by correspondence and to see each other again in the not too distant future.

Chapter Six

At the end of his secondary school education in Toulouse, Babingo obtained the prestigious Latin-Greek baccalaureate which would typically give him the opportunity of furthering his studies in the Humanities in a faculty of the same town. But first, he was filled with the joy of returning to his country for a well-deserved vacation. Once home, the pride of family members and particularly that of Papa Makouta was palpable. Alex Babingo's heart was joyous to see his parents and his girlfriend, Tessa, again.

The airplane which brought back the prodigal child to the country landed directly in

Pointe-Noire, endowed already with an airport which, by the standards of that time, was very modern. The full complement of the family was there. It was a time of big family reunions, characterized by feasts and numerous visits.

Alex took advantage of his stay in the country to participate in many conferences hosted by the students at a period when independence movements were already the order of the day.

Alex Babingo and his friends were particularly active in the groups which were agitating for the immediate independence of Middle Congo, in open opposition to pro-Establishment politicians, defending a referendum that would usher in Franco-African union.

Despite his challenging responsibilities as a student leader, Alex Babingo spared no pains to meet Tessa who, at eighteen years old, had developed into a young woman and a childhood friend for whom he cherished genuine tenderness. He could now discuss with her his plans for a shared life with her.

As Tessa needed to pursue her studies at high school and Babingo himself was going to start his university education far away from the country, nothing was pressing. It was, however, necessary to prepare the grounds for a formal relationship by informing Papa Makouta about his plans. This bone of contention marked the start of a protracted feud between father and son.

"Father, seven years ago, before my departure for Metropolitan France, I formed the habit of going a part of the way to school in the company of a young girl, here, in the country. She's called Tessa. We've maintained a friendly relationship for a long time. Despite the distance which separated us, this relationship has continued and deepened over the years. I'd therefore like to introduce her to you before my return to France."

"Alex, forget this affair, if it's about a girl from a different ethnic group, other than ours, the one I saw her at the station on the day of your departure. Since this girl doesn't belong to our ethnic group, it's out of the question to have any form of relationship with her, let alone a marriage plan."

"Father, nowadays, ethnicity should no longer be an obstacle to marriage. We love each other, the two of us. Tessa's a very good girl."

"She may have all the qualities in the world, she'll still lack knowledge of our totem and therefore, of our taboos which she'll find impossible to respect. I'm asking you to forget this relationship which is likely to provoke the wrath of our ancestors for whom your choice would be tantamount to a betrayal."

Babingo was not in the least convinced by his father's ethnocentric arguments. But it was better to avoid a confrontation with a father who up till then, had sacrificed much to offer his son what he considered the best education possible. It must be acknowledged that, contrary to the erring ways of a good number of his contemporaries, Makouta had jettisoned the idea of a "*deuxième bureau*"[7], a *side chick*, thus devoting his meagre savings to the upbringing of his children. The sacrifice had not been in vain since Babingo came back home with good results.

As a good father much concerned about the future of his son for whom he continued to harbour grandiose ambitions, Makouta asked Alex Babingo about his choice of university programs. While Babingo confessed to have set his sights on linguistic studies in order to arm himself with the knowledge necessary to teach and later to fight for the introduction of national languages in the educational system of his country, his father had a different plan for him. He, Papa Makouta enjoined him to go to medical school.

Another heated discussion flared up between father and son.

---

7   A Francophone African term originating from the Democratic Republic of Congo (DRC), which literally means a "second office," but which, in practice, refers to the extra-conjugal affair with a second partner, other than the recognized spouse. When some men choose to have a third or fourth extra-conjugal relationship, such women are known as *troisième bureau* or *quatrième bureau*, respectively.

"My son, as I pointed out to you before your departure for Metropolitan France, I foresee your future only in medicine, for it's in this profession that you can render the highest service to our community. You'll be a doctor, my son, and nothing else! Do you realize what that would mean to our ethnic group, as students from that locality who have passed the baccalaureate can be counted on the finger tips?"

"Even though I'm aware of the importance of the role of a medical doctor in our community, I don't in the least feel attracted to this career. Certainly, the Latin-Greek baccalaureate combination which I passed with distinction would permit me to register for medicine but my inclination is rather towards linguistics, because I want to fight for the incorporation of national languages into our country's curriculum when it attains full sovereignty."

"What do you want to do with these African vernaculars that you pompously rate as national languages, at a time when only two or three major spoken and written languages dominate the world? We communicate in vernaculars, which are at best local *lingua franca* that no one uses outside our territory. There're more pressing issues than the teaching of local *lingua franca* or mother tongues not to think of the fact that because of their sheer numbers, it would be difficult if not impossible to choose one as an official language."

"Father, it'll be necessary, when the time comes, to differentiate between mother tongues and national languages. Contrary to preconceived ideas, language is an essential component of national identity and of the culture of a people. Also, on the eve of the accession of our country to international sovereignty, we should be prepared to restore all the elements of our culture, starting from our way of expression, which is our first cultural treasure."

"Alex, don't forget that you're the son of a "civilized" and westernized African. We belong an elite group within our clan by virtue of the

fact that we're the only ones to have been formally educated. Teaching national languages in
schools, after the independence of our country,
would only result in pure and simple regression.
That would make our children waste time. To
make it possible for us to communicate among
ourselves and with the external world, our
schools must maintain the teaching of French
as a unique means of written expression and
as official language. We've no time to waste.
Besides, I suspect people like you who advocate
the teaching of non-written national languages
want to establish cheap-rate teaching."

"Dad, you're quite mistaken. There're in the
world numerous languages which are spoken
only by the peoples of these countries. I've
learnt that Icelandic is a language that no other
people in the world speak, except the people
from Iceland. This country only has three hundred and fifty thousand inhabitants. Icelanders
have succeeded in resisting all onslaughts and
their culture has produced globally renowned

writers. Examples abound of countries which jealously maintained the oral and written forms of their languages, in order not to lose their identities, even if they're compelled to learn the so-called international languages in the hope of opening themselves up to the world. Language is the vehicle of all values. Without it, other values are destined to collapse irredeemably. But, Father, since it's your desire and I want to remain your loving and obedient child, I'll register in the medical school as soon as university resumes, on my return to Metropolitan France."

Chapter Seven

Good news as well as bad ones rarely comes alone. While Alex Babingo was meditating on the way to manage the many cases of conflict between his father and himself, he received a desperate telephone call from Ingrid, then in her native Iceland, just two months after their crazy romantic idyll at the beginning of summer, that night, in the "guest house."

What is it that is so important that Ingrid wants to contact him by telephone from such a long distance? In those days, an international telephone call was worth its weight in gold. To communicate by telephone, it was necessary, for the average person to go to a public

place, generally a Postal, Telegraph, and Telephone (PTT) office, wait for one's turn to enter
the booth, and hope that the line would be
good enough to have decent conversations by
telephone.

Ingrid started by apologizing for disturbing
Alex Babingo's vacation. But, because of the
peculiarity of the situation which she was going
through, she desired to meet him very urgently
as soon as he returned to Toulouse.

"What could be the reason for such a
request, when at the time we parted it was only
a question of exchanging letters, from time to
time, especially upon my return from Africa?"

"As I've been trying to explain to you, the
reason is so important and cannot be discussed
on phone. However, I must stress that we
need to talk."

"If it's that important, the very least I expect
you to do is to give me some inkling of it now."

"It's about an unexpected event, important,
and sufficiently serious."

"What's this event?"

A long silence ensued, unending. To break this deafening silence of Ingrid's, Alex Babingo dared drop this fearsome sentence, so far away from his thought, five minutes before. "Could you be pregnant?" After yet a weightier silence, Ingrid let out from the innermost depth of her soul, a yes, mixed with fear and relief at the same time.

"How can one imagine that from one single encounter, such calamitous troubles can happen to me with someone I hardly know?" Alex Babingo grumbled.

If at twenty-one years old, Ingrid was already a major and mature, as is said, Alex Babingo, eighteen years old, just emerging from adolescence, weighed the gravity of his situation. He realized how this stealthy love was going to have a bitter pill to swallow for him and above all, his family, when he informed them about it. There was no way he was going to talk about it with anyone around him. Neither with Papa

Makouta, nor with Tessa. Alex Babingo did not stop torturing his brains over what he considered a rotten luck and at worst a trap into which he had naively fallen.

"At eighteen years old, without any income apart from the allowance which Papa Makouta pays me, where will I find the means to face up to my new status?" he asked himself.

From that moment, his nights were haunted by gloomy ideas; he could only associate his future with hopelessness. For Alex Babingo, the return to Toulouse looked like the Way of the Cross. All the same, he needed to meet Ingrid.

It was in a secluded corner of the café *le Bibent*, this place where they met each other for the first time that the two met again, after a long travel from Reykjavik to Toulouse, undertaken for the occasion by the young woman. With a melancholic countenance, Alex Babingo could not restrain himself from thundering:

"Explain to me what exactly happened. We only met once for the first time for a very brief period and you're re-appearing sixty days later to declare to me I really don't know what. That you're pregnant. That looks like a premeditated affair or a trap, doesn't it? Answer me. Are you sure that you haven't met another man after the single evening we spent together? I'm only a novice in such matters, but because you were no longer a virgin, you must have had relationships with a man before me. Confess that I wasn't the only one."

"If I rushed to call you while you were still on vacation in your country, it was because the gynecologist I consulted had confirmed my fear. I panicked", responded Ingrid.

"Don't be unfair, Alex. You know very well that I hadn't at all set a trap for you. It's absurd to think like that. Yes, I was no longer a young girl jealously guarding her candor when I met you but it's been a long time that I'd sexual relationships with a man. Let me be very frank with you; the last time I'd sexual relationships with a man was when I was a student nurse, on night duty at the university hospital. It's true that I completely forgot myself that night we met. The idea to protect myself totally slipped my mind, mistakenly perhaps, but that's the truth. Come to think of it, the situation is probably serious, but it isn't unmanageable."

"How can you claim that it isn't unmanageable when you know very well that I'm only a student, a first-year student for that matter, without any means, apart from the allowance I receive from my father? How can I present an affair as obscene and as it is shocking to my parents, and more particularly my father, without incurring his wrath? Surely, I'd be exposing myself to some punitive measures from him. I don't want to hear anything more about the story of this pregnancy. That's your baby! Do you hear me?"

"What do you mean by "That's your baby!"? There's no way I'm aborting the pregnancy. Yes, you've no job, but me, I've one. I'm a Social Worker in a hospital for handicapped persons. Even though modest, my income will be enough to meet my needs and to bring up our child. Money isn't the problem."

"It'll be necessary that, for my part, I inform my parents about the situation, unexpected for them too, by giving them the necessary details on the identity of the father of my future child. I can already guess the shock.

"My parents are practicing Lutherans like most Icelanders and very conservative too. It'll therefore be necessary to convince them of the fact that the birth of this being constitutes for me a source of happiness. The idea of giving up on this child has not, for a single second, occurred to me. Your reluctance, accusations or refusal will change nothing. You know now that you're the father of a child who will be born in a few months. I repeat that I haven't had any intimate relationships with anyone else for a long time. I haven't had anything with any other man after our last meeting. Contrary to what you think and despite your fears, our situation is far from being catastrophic."

Having just come out of adolescence himself, Alex Babingo could still not come to terms with his status as a father-to-be. The two young people parted company with Babingo still in a dreadful mood.

Grudgingly, Alex Babingo submitted to the demands of his father and registered at the Medical School of Toulouse which, at that time, attracted numerous African and Asian students because of its great reputation and also for the mild climate of the region. And so commenced the years of hardship for Babingo.

During school sessions, Babingo needed to juggle with elective courses and deferment of examinations in order to maintain himself in what he considered a dead end, a straitjacket, because he neither had the taste nor the inclination for science courses. The battle between his own choice and the demands of Makouta, his father, lasted for four academic years at the end of which Alex Babingo took for the first time and in a resolute fashion, the perilous path of rebellion.

The will to set out on the conquest of his own life and search for authenticity pushed him to abandon medical studies in favour of the Faculty of Arts, and this, without any prior notification to his father. When Makouta eventually heard that his son had abandoned medical studies, he was consumed by anger the depth of which made people imagine his thunderous voice crossing the Atlantic to hit the rebellious child. The result for Alex Babingo was long years of lean times. The allowances that he received regularly from his father were stopped forthwith.

The discovery of the subtleties of Applied Linguistics and the happiness that he experienced in undertaking studies that matched his calling were remarkable. But Babingo was compelled to offer his services as a dishwasher in upscale restaurants of Toulouse. Having what to feed himself with, paying his registration fees at the University, satisfying other requirements associated with his condition as a student were obligations that had to be met.

He confronted life limping through his studies while playing a very active militant role in the local academic chapter of the Federation of African Students in France (FEANF). He discovered, not without some pride, how special this student organization was.

Founded at the beginning of the year 1950 during the Cold War, FEANF played a critical role in the political history of the Continent. And, if its priority goals initially focused on the defense of the material and moral interests of African students sojourning in France, the organization has distinguished itself, since its creation, in the political struggles towards the total independence of French colonies. It was at the forefront of all the struggles for the liberation of colonized peoples.

Justifiably, the leaders and militants of the organization were desirous of personifying the unity of Africa. They wanted to be the pioneers of the construction of a continent unwavering in its movement towards the sovereignty of its constituent States. When, after the Second World War, France began giving its colonial territories a new status, FEANF conducted vigorous campaigns to denounce what its leaders at the time labeled as political deception. For the leaders of the students' organization, the Defferre Reform Act was nothing else than an agenda for the balkanization of Africa. The Act was staunchly resisted in a joint declaration by FEANF and pan- African Trade Unions.

By virtue of this Act which bore the name of the then Minister of Overseas France, colonial power created governing councils endowed with a certain degree of autonomy vis-à-vis Metropolitan France. The Franco-African Community that emerged from the new constitution of 1958 did not only confuse the contemporary

African political class, but met with the fierce and resolute opposition of FEANF which, after the directives of an extraordinary Congress, decided to campaign against the referendum in all the colonies.

In the face of these challenges, the young students living in France, as well as the totality of African youths in the colonies, were by far more demanding than the elitist political class whose moves were limited to the denunciation of racism and manifestations of injustice of which they were more and more conscious victims. It was not long before the systematic opposition of FEANF to what its leaders considered neocolonial maneuvers started to cost the representatives of the movement more and more.

But for a long time, nothing seemed to shake the resolve of this student movement whose existence the authorities of Metropolitan France tolerated. FEANF felt concerned about all that touched the movements of decolonization in Africa and in Asia. The outbreak of the Algerian insurrection and the resultant repression, as well as the assassination of Patrice Lumumba, became moments of great tension between FEANF and all those it called the accomplices of the aggressors. Massive demonstrations followed sensational statements. Above all, leaders and militants were engaged in a large-scale struggle for the promotion of the African homeland, the African continent.

Months passed by, and Ingrid's natural hormonal development soon made it impossible for her to hide her pregnancy. Contrary to Ingrid's fears, her parents were not overly upset when she finally told them about her condition of a mother-to-be. Nor were they unduly worried by the origin of the father. Certainly, they would have preferred, instead of this African, to see their only daughter introduce to them a descendant of the Vikings as her suitor. They would also have preferred to celebrate the union of their daughter with a true-blue Icelander in the national cathedral where all the generations of the family had been wedded. But the thought of becoming grandparents in their lifetime thrilled them above all other considerations.

They insisted on meeting Alex Babingo, but as he felt unequal to the task, he found a thousand and one excuses to decline the invitation. A short while after the birth of his son, Alex Babingo resolved to introduce himself to Ingrid's parents, not because he wanted to gleefully respond to their invitation but, essentially, with the aim of organizing the naming of his son. He had to make him undergo the unique traditional rites of passage of his ethnic group. Alex Babingo had, in effect, become a fervent adept of tradition.

Chapter Eight

The journey to Reykjavik was both desired and dreaded. However, above all, Babingo was in a hurry to know the tiny being, fruit of a one-day romantic act. Travelling from Toulouse to Paris, Alex Babingo had to undertake a long journey with multiple stops of the train at Montauban, Cahors, Brive-la-Gaillarde, Limoges, Vierzon, and finally Paris where he arrived exhausted. With the train ticket to Copenhagen via Cologne in his hand, he still had to wait for some hours again before boarding another which would take him to the Danish capital to continue his peregrination.

After a long wait in the Gare du Nord lobby, Alex Babingo saw the Paris-Cologne train arrive on the platform around 5:30 in the evening. He sank into the first seat of a coach in the second class, until he became aware that he was occupying a seat different from the one he had been allotted. He moved from there to the right couchette where he placed his travelling bag on the shelf above him. It was already dark when the train conductor announced their impending arrival in Cologne.

Having crossed the maze of this huge station, Babingo managed to reach the Cologne-Copenhagen platform in good time. The departure time was announced for 10 o'clock in the evening. Overhearing a conversation between two travelers, he learnt that this train had the habit of leaving late. But Babingo had become a regular user of station lobbies. He therefore chose to use the time to stave off his hunger by crunching the cheese bread which he had bought at the café opposite the lobby. The Borealis City train run by the German railway arrived at the platform around 10:20 pm.

Babingo was among the many passengers who were hurrying up to reach their cabins as he wove his way through the crowd to quickly find his couchette. There were six stacked and well-arranged beds with matching duvets for passengers inside the cabin. In the still icy night of the Scandinavian countryside at the beginning of spring, the powerful Borealis locomotive cut through adverse and foggy winds with great speed, haughtily ignoring the intermediary stations to stop only at Kolding, and later at Odense where many passengers disembarked, some because they had arrived at their destination and others to take a connecting train to other destinations.

It was 10 o'clock in the morning when the Borealis arrived finally at Copenhagen station. Alex Babingo had some difficulty overcoming a fatigue worsened by the intense cold which made him miss the beautiful spring of Toulouse, the Pink City. After a train journey of a more than twenty-four hours, Babingo began another lap to the distant and isolated country called Iceland. He covered more than two thousand kilometers by sea, one thousand and seventy-nine nautical miles, in addition, before reaching Reykjavik. In those days, one needed to endure three and a half days of travel by sea on a ferry boat departing from Hanstholm Port.

Alex Babingo went back to the cabin assigned him by the young steward dressed in white, stationed on the deck, who was welcoming passengers, with a conventional smile on his lips. As the first to arrive, the young passenger could choose in a windowless cabin, one of the four wrought iron beds stacked and tightly screwed in the hole of the ship. He sat down on the bed at the lowest level of the row near the bathroom to which he could easily have access. As a real floating house, the ferryboat had luxurious cabins, a gourmet restaurant, a cafeteria, and many entertainment rooms.

Alex Babingo was content with going to the cafeteria where he could eat fish soup as much as he wanted and sample sandwiches stuffed with smoked mutton. With a humming from its siren to announce its departure, the ferryboat headed in the direction of Shetland Islands, crossed Faroe Islands, magnificent sites where passengers could view the beautiful and majestic fjords, before arriving finally at Seydisfjordur, in the east of Reykjavik.

With his head already filled with the names of places more or less difficult to remember, Alex Babingo would later discover and experience a country without trees, but offering a unique sight to the world of colours and an environment of rare serenity. Alex Babingo saw on the platform of Seydisfjordur a silhouette wrapped in a red coat and with her blond hair battling with a recalcitrant wind: Ingrid signaled her presence to reassure her visitor.

After a long and silent hug, Ingrid went with Alex towards the bus which would convey them to Reykjavik. Filled with emotion and paralyzed by this difficult meeting, both necessary and inevitable, Ingrid and Alex did not, for some time, know what to say to each other. It was almost like eternity. Suddenly, Ingrid broke the silence: "He resembles you a lot, you know". As if they emanated from the depth of her soul, these few words came awash with spasmodic tears that she could hardly contain. Not knowing how to respond, Alex held Ingrid's left hand while the bus headed for the city-centre of Reykjavik.

Babingo did not stop thinking about how he would react at the crucial moment, when, faced with reality, he would see the new-born baby in the presence of Ingrid's parents. In which language would he express himself, he, who did not know a single word of the Icelandic language and whose spoken English was rather poor? He remembered, quite happily, that during their very first encounter, Ingrid had told him about her father, who had been a student at the Sorbonne University in Paris, some thirty years earlier.

Another cause of concern for Babingo was the question of what the future for Ingrid would be now that she has become a mother. Frankly put, did he envisage establishing a union later with her upon the completion of his studies? And how would he respond to such a question if it was posed? It was without any particular formality that, as good Scandinavians, Ingrid's parents welcomed the visitor in their small house situated at the exit of the city-center.

"My name is Jön Einarsson. And this is my wife, Eleina. Please, call me Jön, for according to the customs here in Iceland, people are called by their first names."

"Alex is my Christian first name and Babingo my family name."

The exchange of some rather brief civilities over, Babingo met his child, so to speak, then a twelve-day-old boy. The emotion in this young man of barely 20 years old himself, who had become a father, was tangible. After putting Alex Babingo in the room adjacent to the baby's, his hosts invited him to a family meal. Smoked mutton, served with "flat-brand" (a type of pancake cooked in the embers) and marinated fish. He was also treated to some "kjutsupa", a beef stew of incomparable delight.

From the word go, Alex Babingo informed his hosts about the purpose of his visit. If he came soon after the birth of his son, it was because he needed to make the child undergo the rituals peculiar to his lineage. It was crucial that he should communicate with the soul of the new-born baby. Every day, Alex Babingo has to whisper into the baby's right ear the traditional first name which he would bear but which would only be revealed on the ninth day of his birth. By simply calling out this first name into the baby's ear, Alex Babingo would be inviting the spirits of the ancestors who surrounded the baby to welcome him into the midst of both the living and the invisible, because he would automatically become one of theirs, a full-fledged member of the lineage.

If Alex Babingo failed to repeat this first name to the newborn, should the baby unfortunately pass away before the day of his naming, his soul would stand the risk of roaming eternally, without being able to lay claim to any lineage. His soul would forever be led astray and become lost. Among the other rituals planned for the naming ceremony were first, the shaving of the skull of the tiny being, and second, a circumcision within the shortest possible time but, at the very latest, within thirty days after his birth.

"If it were possible for me, I would equally be buckling down to inculcating into him right from his young age, the little that I know about the values of our culture, starting with our language which seems to have been annihilated by another culture, thus rendering us consenting deracinated beings. The tragedy is that I'm myself a perfect specimen of *those who have abandoned their language and their spirituality in order to practice those of others*. Totally disarmed, they are *incapable of transmitting anything about their* spirituality to their descendants. In short, I dream of the day when I would be able to speak my mother tongue with my son and later with all my future children."

A long dialogue started between Jön Einarsson and Babingo on habits and customs, African beliefs, and residual Icelandic customs.

"I find it cruel to strip the poor baby of the sparse downy hairs which protect his frail head," declared Jön Einarsson. "I also do not support the idea of seeing him mangled in the first months of his coming into the world. In my opinion, those were very well-respected customs but are totally outmoded in our days. For the others, I'm in perfect agreement with you."

Babingo cared little about these views, determined as he was to subject the baby to the initiation rites of his ancestors.

"You've your own beliefs, some of which continue to exist and we've ours."

"You're right. We also in the past used to worship gods some of whom were belligerent, while others were peaceful and life-giving. Thor, the god associated with iron, was the most popular in ancient Iceland. Some animals such as the crow and the horse played a very important role in ancient Scandinavian beliefs. The horse was a sacrificial animal par excellence, which made it forbidden for us to eat its flesh. Our magicians and especially our sorceress-prophetesses enjoyed great prestige.

"But it's been a long since we disavowed almost all these pagan beliefs and those which subsist are very few. They're only practiced by an insignificant fraction of our people. For example, we've here in Iceland the *Huldufolk*, or the hidden people. More or less benevolent supernatural creatures, the *Huldufolk* are legendary beings, some sort of elves, trolls, and other reputed invisible characters who live mainly on our mountain tops. People claim it's in the rocks and mountains that they choose to build their towns, the *Alagablettur*.

"As regards the choice of surnames and first names, our naming system is conventional and very simple. The family name of a person is formed from the first name of his or her father. Thus, the ancestral name of Ingrid isn't Einarsson but Jöndöttir.

"It does appear strange that in this day and age, you still believe in the existence of invisible beings. In fact, it is, I repeat, a tiny minority of Icelanders, notably the mediums who claim to see the *Huldufolk* and even to communicate with them.

"Even though most Icelanders scarcely accord any interest to what has become a folk-lore and relics of a bygone past, the abodes of these beings are still preserved today. In certain regions of the country, the layouts of roads are carefully done to avoid the places where the *Huldufolk* lived, according to some people, in order not to destroy their dwelling-place. In reality, I believe that it has a lot more to do with people not wanting to offend the sensibilities of the people of the concerned regions than according credit to this belief.

"All these are isolated cases because nowadays, the vast majority of Icelanders believe only in what is visible and palpable to them, even if I must admit that in Iceland, we live in a country where nature is unpredictable. The *Huldufolk* do not haunt the nights of Icelanders. But then, if I understand you, the daily life of your people still remains apparently dictated by these numerous beliefs of another epoch. On the other hand, I understand you perfectly when you wish to be able to restore some elements of your culture and more particularly your national languages.

"After having known an *age of peace*, Iceland experienced what was called an *interminable night*, term evocative of the period during which it was led by five great families who tore one another into pieces. The result was total anarchy which benefitted foreign countries. But, despite several hundred years of foreign tutelage, the Icelandic language has remained the written and spoken language here; it has remained the only official and instructional language.

"Admittedly, the geographical isolation and important culture of writing have sustained the resistance of Iceland to exogenous linguistic influence. That has allowed the exceptional preservation of the original language in its written and oral versions."

"We must preserve our beliefs so that they can support our very existence, that is the unity of being, the convergence of the physically dead and the living," Babingo stressed.

"Circumcision must be performed, preferably, within the first thirty days of his birth so that the baby experiences the least suffering possible. It is a crucial stage in an individual's life. This rite of consecration confers on him a masculine identity and the unrestrained right of entry into the company of men once he reaches puberty."

Chapter Nine

The birth of a child occasions well-defined rituals as for example, the secret burial of the placenta at a carefully chosen spot outside the abode of the child's parents. At this spot will be planted a fruit tree to convey the wish that the mother would bear as many children as the tree bore fruits. Unable to ground his choice of name on the basis of traditional rites, Babingo acted on his intuition by giving a befitting first name, guided by the little he had appropriated from his mother tongue. He named him Mwana- yu Kikimayô or simply Kikimayô, which, in essence, meant child of astonishment. This first name was whispered into the ears of the baby from the first moment of Babingo's arrival in Reykjavik.

Ingrid's family was willing to concede and accept the traditional first name given by Alex Babingo to his son, but this choice was going to clash with the stiff resistance of the municipal authorities of Reykjavik. In Iceland, it was out of the question to record in the national register a first name which did not feature on the list of the three thousand authorized first names. It became necessary then to find a compromise between the respect of the tradition which Babingo treasured so much and the demands of the Icelandic registry office.

It was necessary that the traditional rites be subjected to the laws of the country where the child was born. In Icelandic language, Kikimayô was named Didrik Alexson. This way, the first name of the father followed by the suffix "son" became the ancestral name of the child. Nonetheless, by the spirit of openness and compromise, the new-born baby bore Kikimayô as second given name.Compromise is necessary for the maintenance of the dialogue of cultures.

While Babingo was preparing to return to Toulouse after an eight-week stay, Jön Einarsson had a private discussion with him. As a good father concerned about the future of his daughter, Jön wanted to know Alex's intentions in this respect. Did Babingo plan building a common future with his daughter?

"Alex, what are your plans for Ingrid now that you have Didrik Alexson Kikimayô?"

"Though your question is relevant, it seems premature to me. Before the end of my studies, I cannot promise anything."

Not wanting to shock his interlocutor, the young man corrected his error and promised to live up to his responsibilities, even if his status as a student would not permit him to do much. He added: "For the rest, the future will guide us."

Disappointed at Alex Babingo's rather vague response, Ingrid's father could not hide his disappointment. Besides, he did not know if his daughter would be able to live with this young man from a very faraway country. If yes, was he going to separate her from her family? As a result, when Babingo and Jön were parting company, farewell and other compliments exchanged between the two men were limited and rather cold.

On his return from Reykjavik, during his stock-taking, Alex recalled in turns his extraordinary journey, his equally extraordinary stay in Iceland, and the strangeness of his situation. Due to the peculiar circumstances of his presence in Ingrid's country, he had feared a cold reception. But that was not the case. On the contrary, the discussions he had had were marked by geniality, simplicity, and generosity, even if at the time of his departure, his rapport with Jön had been cold.

The intercultural exchange between the two men was not easy at the beginning. If there had been skirmishes with respect to beliefs, the fiction was devoid of rudeness but rather characterized by remarkable civility.

During his stay in Reykjavik, Alex Babingo would very much have loved to have the time to discuss with Ingrid their future plans centering on little Kikimayô. But given the precariousness of his impecunious student status, could he have made a commitment? Consequent upon his disagreement with his father because of his choice of studies and the profession which he should practice, Papa Makouta decided to pull the plug on him by cutting off his allowance. And, since then, Alex Babingo worked part-time at the postal sorting center, doing a night job which, though not particularly rewarding provided him with an income sufficient meet his basic needs.

It was not easy for him to juggle the life of a student with that of an employee, but did he have a choice? He had much less of a choice with the birth of Kikimayô as he was obliged to make a contribution, even if symbolic, to the upkeep of the child. He knew that Ingrid's job would make it possible for her to meet the needs of the child all alone, but he insisted on sharing with her the financial and moral responsibility that the maintenance of this child entailed.

Chapter Ten

Beyond its emotional dimension, Babingo's journey to Iceland reinforced his ambition to decolonize the educational system in his country. He discovered that Iceland, which suffered for many centuries the successive domination of its two neighbours, Norway and Denmark, had been able to resist acculturation.

This country, whose discovery and human habitation date back to the ninth century only, invented Althing, an assembly considered to be the oldest parliament in the world. The country experienced a period of independence which lasted close to four centuries. But the internecine conflicts and the inter-clan wars shattered this independence. It led to the weakening of the country which initially became, a Norwegian colony from the middle of the thirteenth century. Then came the abolition, in the sixteenth century, of the Kalmar Union, comprising Denmark, Sweden, and Norway. This break of alliance brought in its wake the domination of Iceland by the kingdom of Denmark for more than five hundred years. The Danish kingdom did not only take over commerce, but also imposed on the country the Protestant reform. Then followed the decline of the Icelandic people marked by an intense poverty. That notwithstanding, these people succeeded in developing a unique culture.

The evangelization of the island was not easy, because as pagans, Icelanders believed in Nordic mythology. The first missions failed dismally. And it was only under the threat of a massacre of the rebels impervious to conversion that Icelanders accepted to be evangelized to avoid a pogrom and a religious war. But the

Norwegian colonizers had to make do with a conversion mixed with a local flavour. Icelanders insisted on the preservation of some of their traditions and the continuation of the private practice of paganism.

The country's era of revival commenced with the struggle for independence, inspired by the wind of change which was then blowing across the whole of Europe. Initiated in the nineteenth century by agitations for autonomy, national sovereignty was only attained in 1944, accidentally so to speak, following the invasion of Denmark, Iceland's suzerain country, by Nazi Germany. Secession from Denmark was unilaterally approved by almost the totality of Icelandic people.

And yet... despite more than seven hundred years of foreign domination, Icelanders had jealously kept alive the essential elements of their culture: authenticity in their mode of expression, authenticity in their manner of naming themselves and, to a certain extent, their eating habits.

Icelandic people had retained their official and national language, as well as that of the school system since the dawn of time, from kindergarten to the university.

The Icelandic people had always defended their language against the invasion of words and expressions coming from outside. Instead of submitting to international neologism and technical terms, Icelandic language *tamed* them. Thus, the telephone is called *simi:* "line that speaks"; passport *vegabref* meaning "road paper" in Icelandic, and many other words nicely icelandicized. Emboldened by the Icelandic experience, Babingo had become aware of the necessity to act in order to restore the dignity, first to the Téké people, and then, to the entire country.

In three years, Babingo would finish his studies. He wished to embark upon linguistic research, after his university education, his ambition being to promote the introduction of the teaching of national languages in the educational system and adult literacy. He would restrict himself first to his country and later, acting in concert with other linguists, to the totality of the African continent. What a wild dream, what a utopia! However, for Alex Babingo, dream was life. "Without utopia, no progress is possible," he said.

His other dream was to see Kikimayô, alias Didrick, tread the soil of his ancestors, take root there and why not, play the role of the head of a lineage and work for the restoration of the cultural heritage of his community. At first, he had difficulty adjusting to the Icelandic name of his son. But Babingo understood that Icelanders cherished their custom which had eventually acquired the force of law. The children born in their territory bear their first names exclusively featuring on the list of Icelandic registry office. A demand for identity which he approved.

Babingo had given a first name to his son without the knowledge of his own father. This was not to defy the patriarch, but because he Babingo was afraid of clashing with him. He was convinced that Makouta did not know anything about his new status as a young father. He thought he would be able to hide it from him for as long as possible.

But such a thought failed to reckon with the numerous visits that Makouta made regularly to his village to consult the oracles before any undertaking. This time, he went there for something entirely different from what the old and great healer, Nga Babatolé, was going to reveal to him. As always, after having made some incantations, Babatolé the soothsayer threw some kola nuts on a mat spread before him and asked Makouta to take one from them, then another and finally a third one which he mixed in the heap.

Before responding to Makouta's concerns, Nga Babatolé asked him a question with a surprising revelation.

"Makouta, your eldest son is presently in a faraway country, isn't he?"

"Yes, what has happened to him," demanded a visibly perplexed Makouta from old Babatolé.

"Nothing bad," replied the old healer "but your son has had a child with an *nzugu* woman. Fortunately, he has given the child a first name that conforms to our customs and unique to our clan. Without doubting it, this first name which he gave almost matches the predictions of the oracle, even if he has had to add another first name to respect the customs of the country where the child was born."

Makouta could not believe his ears. First of all, he thought the old healer, having probably drunk too much *dolo*, the local wine, was fabricating stories. He remained incredulous but thanked the old healer after making a mental note of the other predictions and paying something for the offerings prescribed by the deities.

He resolved, however, to question Alex Babingo to find out more about this curious revelation made by Nga Babatolé: the existence of a child which his own son was allegedly hiding from him. Faced with the obvious, Alex Babingo could not dodge the issue. Thus, Kikimayô officially entered the family, thanks to the revelation of the old healer. However, Makouta, who could not tolerate the fact that his son abandoned medical studies for an "adventurous" specialization in linguistics could not stomach this new offence.

Nonetheless, to make the best of a bad situation, Makouta accepted Kikimayô's arrival as a gift from his ancestors who seemed favourably disposed to the arrival of this little being, this new addition. He had no idea what life was going to offer Alex Babingo, the rebellious child.

Chaper Eleven

At the very beginning of independence of Francophone African countries, expulsion measures initiated by the French authorities were applied to students. Most often these expulsion measures were at the express request of the governments of the respective countries of origin of African students. Some went underground in order to escape the tragic fate which sometimes awaited them in their countries.

Prohibitions increased each time FEANF applied for authorization to organize a protest meeting. The repression was such that a student movement advocated the boycott of French universities. But this proposal was

not supported by most. A certain number of
expelled students had therefore felt compelled
to seek refuge in Eastern European universities.
Those who had chosen to remain in Metropolitan France continued with the struggle for
what they called a genuine decolonization of
their countries.

Then, in 1959, it was with unanimity
that the members of the local Committee of
FEANF appointed Alex Babingo to represent
the Toulouse chapter at the 15th Congress of
the Federation to be held in Paris. True to type,
Alex made time to dissect the foundational act
of the organization as well as the house rules of
the Congress. As expected, the main items captured on the agenda of this meeting centered
on the living conditions of African students in
France and on the question of decolonization.

The cultural activities of the Federation of
students were rather focused on the publication
treating general questions such as *"the existence*

of an authentic culture of the black world or the *"pro-motion of the African continental homeland."*

Babingo noted, not without some disappointment, that essential and concrete issues such as the incorporation of national languages into the educational system were not a priority for the Congress. He swore to remedy these grave lacunae. He saw his chance when the Chairperson of the Congress asked delegates if they had any modifications to make to the agenda.

The delegate of the Toulouse branch demanded that an in-depth debate on the possibility of creating, on a more or less long-term basis, an African language. A resolution should, according to him, be addressed to the autonomous governments that emerged from the Defferre Reform Act and to other African governments for the establishment of structures that promote the incorporation of national languages into the curriculum and educational practices.

After endless debates on the appropriateness of deliberating on such a topic, the Congress agreed to devote some minutes of discussion to it. Babingo was thus able to put forward his arguments, and this was followed by rather epic discussions between resolute opponents and himself. He contended:

"While I admit that issues such as the organization of our lives as students here in France and decolonization are of the highest priority, I am equally persuaded that the restoration of our cultural heritage – at the top of which I place teaching in African national languages – should already be engaging our attention at the moment our countries are on the verge of gaining international sovereignty. Our languages are the vehicle of our cultures and our way of thinking. Cheikh Anta Diop was right in advocating African linguistic unity after demonstrating in an impressive manner that *African languages can be utilized in the exact sciences and philosophy.*"

"At a time when political organizations and labour unions of Africa, Camara observed, "count on our action to accelerate the process of the total liberation of our countries and the eradication of apartheid everywhere and by all means possible, you are asking us to devote precious hours of our deliberations to the question of national languages.

"You know, Babingo, that in each of our countries we speak about sixty if not more vernaculars and, with regionalism dominating almost everywhere, all the ethnic groups will demand that their vernaculars or mother tongues be raised to the status of national languages."

"By advocating the incorporation of national languages into the educational system, I remain aware of the fact that for the time being, the speaking of the French language will permit us to understand one another and to partially resolve the communication problems confronting our peoples within the same country. It isn't, at all, a question of raising the sixty maternal languages spoken in a country to the status of national languages. It's also necessary not to confuse national languages with mother tongues.

"If, within the same country all the citizens can communicate in two or three national languages, they would understand and know one another better. Moreover, the courses taught in school in national languages would make it possible for our children to achieve significant progress in terms of the comprehension of concepts and the formation of their own young minds. Teaching in national languages would certainly contribute in helping them to safeguard and operationalize their cultural identity."

"We already have a language," retorted Epéna, "the French language which allows us to communicate with virtually one third of the peoples of the planet.

"Of what use would the knowledge of national languages be to us outside each of our territories? Besides, that would most likely slow down the learning of the French language at the elementary school level and afterwards, studies in universities and high-level specialized scientific and professional institutions."

"Far from being an obstacle to the learning of French, the teaching in national languages which, besides, should become our official languages, would give school children a wider capacity of exposure, which as we all know, will easily make them multilingual, or at least bilingual.

"Anyway, it is necessary to recall that our administrative authorities who claim to be close to the people communicate in a foreign language with the masses who, in their over-whelming majority, do not understand the message being put across. Without formal training in our national languages in Africa, we will forever suffer from acculturation."

"I request," interjected Camara, "that we defer the examination of this issue till our next Congress. Babingo objected to Camara's proposal. He insisted:

"One can only learn easily when one understands. But then, a number of you certainly remember the pain you suffered when trying to understand the teacher, on the day of your entry into school. You surely have not forgotten how you were hanging on to every word of the teacher who was trying to transmit knowledge in a language that you did not understand. You needed to make special efforts to memorize hard; fortunately, that was possible because of your young age."

"As you should admit," retorted Dossou, "we pulled through it, since today, we can all express ourselves in a common international language."

"Yes, we pulled through it but at the cost of many rejects who, on the way, had to drop out of school. Once more, I don't recommend the rejection of the teaching of the French language. We must be able to learn to standardize writing and speaking of our national languages."

The discussions went on interminably between Babingo and those opposed to his proposal. Those who accepted the validity of the request of the student of linguistics and those who were indifferent to it contented themselves with the verbal sparring duels of the two opposing camps.

The Executive Board of Congress ended the discussion abruptly by constituting an *ad hoc* committee charged with writing a recommendation addressed to the African political leaders of the time to ensure the restoration of our cultures. They insisted more particularly on the necessity to legislate, at the opportune time, for the choice of national languages to be incorporated into the educational system not only for the good of school children, but also that of illiterates.

If he was aware of the fact that the vague recommendation of FEANF's Congress was like burying the issue, Babingo was still relieved to see his proposal documented and addressed formally to the territorial governments then in the process of formation in Francophone African countries. Small consolation, it is true, for Babingo was dreaming of a more radical continent-focused decision in order to put an end to a frustration that was becoming more and more intolerable.

In reality, one had to wait for several decades for Africa, notably francophone Africa, for the elitist political class to become aware of the imperative of making the instruction in national languages compulsory, from a very young age. Awareness is one thing; the political will to act is another.

Chapter Twelve

The hunt for African students who were leaders or simple militants of FEANF was in full swing when Alex Babingo returned to Toulouse after the Congress. Alex was hounded for belonging to the group of representatives who had signed the declaration condemning African leaders pushing the people to vote for the new Constitution of the Franco-African community. Furthermore, he made himself more conspicuous towards the end of the 15th Congress by refusing from then on to be called by his first name, Alex. It was necessary to replace his name with another, an authentic Bantu name. He called himself Intu Ngolo. Thenceforth, his name became Intu Ngolo Babingo.

In order to ward off the threat of expulsion, would he have to leave Toulouse for one of the socialist countries where some of his friends had found refuge? Would he need to go and support the young Republic of Guinea or Mali in the name of African solidarity? "Revolutionary" Guinea had welcomed many militants of the famous African students' movement then in a strained relationship with the French authorities of the time and especially with those of their own countries of origin.

Would he have to leave for one of the countries of Northern Europe committed to active neutrality, and opening up to leaders of Third-World organizations struggling for the independence of their countries? He even for a moment considered Iceland, a country with which he found himself connected thenceforth. Didn't Didrik Alexson, alias Mwana Yu Kikimayô, come from his own blood? However, he changed his mind very quickly after weighing the pros and cons of the choices available to him.

Intu Ngolo Babingo finally chose to return to African soil. Better still, he opted for a return to his mother's village of origin. This refuge in a country which he had left as an adolescent and particularly, in a village where he had never set foot was considered a heresy by his friends. Known henceforth as Intu Ngolo Babingo, he was perceived as a crank when he revealed to those close to him that he wanted to return home to standardize the *Téké* alphabet, its vocabulary and grammar, stressing that his mother tongue happened to be one of the major languages of the country. In the opinion of all, this choice appeared as audacious as it was utopic.

With his degree of advanced studies in linguistics in hand, Intu Ngolo Babingo had no doubt of the appropriateness of his choice. He felt sufficiently armed to quickly appropriate the basics of his mother tongue which he strongly desired thenceforth to standardize and to elevate to the rank of one of the national languages. But already, the journey looked forebodingly long, very long, punctuated with multiple trials and tribulations.

From Paris airport, Intu Ngolo Babingo arrived at night in a sleeping Leopoldville[8], the Belgian Congo capital which, at that time of the day, only owed its semblance of life to the pallid light emanating from the street lamps of the big avenues. It was at day break in a city that was hardly awake that the adventurer followed the path to the riverside to discretely board the boat which took him to the other bank.

Assembled there were passengers draped in outfits of shimmering colours, who were going towards the landing stage in an apparently controlled disorder, some carrying on their heads jute bags containing off-season tomatoes, others

---

8   Now known as Kinshasa, the capital of the Democratic Republic of Congo (DRC).

with bales of wax cloths, freshly manufactured by the Matoto factory.

Intu Ngolo Babingo dreaded coming across a member of his family who, upon recognizing him, could not be prevented from informing his parents of the presence of their son in the country.

Still incognito, the passenger boarded the bus going towards the north of the country, through unwelcoming tracks. The vehicle never ceased zigzagging on roads full of potholes whose location the driver seemed to know about from experience and memorization. For, he avoided them with so much skill.

At each of the numerous stops, at villages with evocative names dotted on the route, passengers embarked or disembarked. These brief stops offered some of the passengers on the bus the opportunity to buy food items which they considered to be cheap. Sellers of bananas, pineapples, avocados, fat countryside rats, and other fresh game meat, ran behind the bus which, to stop without disturbing a traffic flow particularly heavy at this time of the day, encroached upon a part of the verge.

These stopovers also offered Intu Ngolo Babingo the opportunity to temporarily leave the shaky seat of the bus on which he has been sitting during this unending journey. After many hours of drive, the bus stopped on the bank of River Ndjiri. Intu Ngolo was one of the passengers who crossed it.

It was with another boat that he arrived at Odiba, the village of origin of his mother Mamatouka. As soon as Babingo stated the identity of his mother's lineage, the first stroller who seemed to be waiting for the arrival of boats, quickly showed him the path leading to the hut of old Makolondinga, the representative of the lineage of the Imanos. Babingo announced his presence and asked a young man stationed before the gate of the compound to inform the old wise man of his presence. Mpiri turned out to be both the nephew and loyal assistant of old Makolondinga.

"My name is Intu Ngolo Babingo and I would like to meet the head of the lineage of the Imanos, here in Odiba."

"How do I announce your presence more precisely in order for the venerable head of lineage to situate you in the family?"

"I'm the eldest son of Mamakouta, whom he gave out in marriage to Paul Makouta of the neighboring village, some years ago."

After the guest has been served a bowl of water as a welcoming gesture, Old Makolondinga, still stretched on his bamboo bed, asked his assistant to seat Intu Ngolo Babingo on the stool, facing him.

Since Babingo did not understand the *Téké* language, Mpiri had to serve as interpreter between him and the head of lineage.

"Then, you're the son of Mamakouta, Anlabo's daughter, whom we gave out in marriage almost thirty seasons ago. It was the period blessed by our ancestors during which our forests were full of caterpillars. We harvested from them more than we needed to bridge the gap.

"You must be tired after many hours of driving on the bus and crossing the river. How is Mamakouta? And her husband? Did they give you tobacco for me?"

"Venerable Head of lineage, I'm not coming from Nkuna, Babingo said referring to Brazzaville, for such was its original appellation, by which the Imanos continued to call this city. It was, besides, the capital of French Equatorial Africa. I've travelled from afar to reach here. Neither Mamakouta, nor my father knows as yet that I'm here. I'm coming to the village to draw knowledge from the sources of our culture. I'm here to learn to speak a perfect Téké and later, with the help of the other sons of this community, create an alphabet and the rules of a standard language."

"This is an excellent step that you want to take, my son. It's about an initiation into the mysteries of the Téké language. But, as you must know, we do not take any initiative here without first consulting our ancestors. I'll submit your request to Igulaguo, the great soothsayer, the only one able to reveal to us the decision of our ancestors. You must arm yourself with patience and be ready to remain in the village for as long as necessary."

"Venerable Head of lineage, I'm ready to stay for the time that is required."

"For now, it'll be necessary to put you somewhere in the compound."

Old Makolondinga's compound was a collection of many round huts of straw roofs, built with mud, raw mud bricks made from clay moulded with water and mixed with straw and cow dung.

In the land of the Téké, the construction of a hut was a collective enterprise in which all members of the family and even neighbours participated, for in Odiba village, there were neither artisans nor specialized masons.

The courtyard was the venue for most of the domestic activities and discussions held at night to resolve issues. There were also the imposing hut of the family head, those of his wives, bachelors' huts, those earmarked as guests' quarters, and those where fetishes were kept.

The hen-house and sheep-fold were at the far end, in the right wing of the compound.

Old Makolondinga ordered Mpiri to put Babingo in the hut reserved for unmarried guests.

To get to this abode, the new arrival had to pass through a door made of straw and clod placed against the wall to create a passage for him. Inside was a bamboo bed covered with a bicoloured mat. Intu Ngolo Babingo put his small suitcase by the bed. Two stretched iron lines fixed on the wall across the room were used for hanging clothes. Majestically positioned near the front door was a wooden stool made of teak.

A candle was found placed in the middle of the room, in a clay bowl and not far from there, a box of matches which seemed to be waiting quietly for the night to contribute to the lighting of Intu Ngolo Babingo's new abode. Daily life looked special and in all aspects, different from that which Babingo led in Toulouse, far, very far from Odiba. In particular, when the fishing season comes, he will have to be initiated into it, first by accompanying Mpiri, an expert fisherman, who will teach him to catch fish with bare hands in the river. He will also need to get used to eating the dishes of the region.

Intu Ngolo Babingo seemed to submit himself willingly to his condition of a villager. In the compound, he was obliged to live in the bachelors' quarters. He only had direct contact with the head of the lineage and Mpiri. Whenever it became necessary, he participated in the reconstruction works of the straw roofs of neighbours' huts, as was the custom in the village.

But as one would expect, he could not escape a little crisis of dysentery that got him bedridden for some days. He was healed with a medicinal infusion brought out straight from the numerous jars which populated old Makolondinga's courtyard. Some days later, the decision of Igulaguo the soothsayer was made known.

Old Makolondinga informed Babingo that the ancestors had granted his request. They gave their consent for him to be taught the Téké language in its subtleties, on the condition that he accepts to make a commitment: that of equally acquiring the science of the healer.

The soothsayer revealed that the ancestors had seen in Intu Ngolo Babingo the descendant who would provide the qualities required to replace the old healer of the village, when, one day, the old man would embark on the long journey to rejoin the ancestors. It had become urgent to identify a promising child of the lineage, capable of protecting the members of the family from the attacks of witches and other malevolent powers.

"The great village healer to whom I'll take you when the moment comes will finalize the conditions of your learning. Concerning the knowledge of the language, I'll be responsible for organizing sessions based on a tested method, but I repeat to you, you must arm yourself with patience and also be alert."

"I don't in the least feel that I've the heart of a healer, which corresponds to the medical career that Makouta, my father, wanted to force me to accept. After my high school studies in Metropolitan France, he had wanted me to enter the medical school. But then, I've no passion for this profession. My only vocation was and still remains that of devoting myself to teaching, for I'm desirous of dedicating my life to transmitting knowledge in the national language, preferably in Téké language, to the young generation. I've oriented my studies in

Mputu towards the science of language and languages."

"The medical doctor heals common and visible sicknesses. The science of healing demands a very vast knowledge in natural medicine and the occult," retorted the chief of lineage. The healer is both a magician and a soothsayer. He holds a power incomparable to that of the medical doctor. Besides, as well as I have just notified you of, it is the spirits of our ancestors that have ordered that you be imperatively guided toward the learning of the science of healing before handing to you the secrets of the Téké language. You'll find it difficult to extricate yourself from the demands of the spirits. It's your destiny, in a way. With respect to the results of the consultation, you've no other choice than compliance, because of the danger of incurring the wrath of our deities. My duty as the leader of our lineage commands me to spare you from such a calamity."

Chapter Thirteen

At the first crow of the cock, starting from the morrow of the day Babingo escaped from the treacherous dysentery, old Makolondinga led him to the hut of Nga Mpandu, the old healer who would initiate him into the secrets of plants and other objects of proven beneficial value. Remarkably spacious, the hut of the healer was situated in the center of a compound which had no less than half a dozen others.

"I bow down to salute you, powerful sooth-sayer, healer and enlightened magus," declared Makolondinga, upon his entry into this cavern of a place, bending his whole height as a sign of reverence, with Babingo, who was in tow and as on cue, making the same gesture.

When they penetrated into this obscure space that served as reception room for patients, Intu Ngolo Babingo found himself in front of a man with an imperturbable face, painted in a sort of red and white clay, with red eyes, his neck bearing charms made of parrot feathers. His neck also bore the horn of an animal whose species the young man could not guess. He noticed, laid on bare ground, the pots containing concoctions ready to be served, statuettes each as strange as the other, a very big mirror, surrounded with cowries and with diverse objects, all conveying the certain presence of ancestral spirits with which the soothsayer-healer probably communed on a daily basis.

Seated on a mat, the edges of which were packed full of amulets, the old healer welcomed his visitors with amiability.

"Hail you, Makolondinga, worthy son of the Imano lineage. To what do I owe the pleasure of your visit so very early in the morning?"

"Venerable Nga Mpandu, I'm here to submit a case of revelation. Our ancestors have named Intu Ngolo Babingo, son of Mamakouta, whom I bring here, as the one who must play the role of the protector of the lineage; the one who, thanks to the science of healing, will be capable of shielding us from potential malevolent acts of sorcerers and other calamities. Having come from afar, he would like to be initiated into the secrets of our language. The spirits have accepted his request, on the condition that in return, he complies with their demand, that of complementing his knowledge of language with that of a healer. I'm bringing you Intu Ngolo Babingo in order that you teach him your vast knowledge, recognized throughout hundreds of villages and even beyond."

"Worthy representative of the Imano lineage, you know that one becomes a healer after learning the necessary procedures from an experienced healer, or by submitting to the will of the ancestors who appoint their candidate, or as a form of inheritance. The case of Intu Ngolo Babingo seems to derive from the verdict of the spirits of your ancestors. It wouldn't be a surprise to me if you were to tell me that he's fallen sick since his nomination by the oracle."

"Indeed, Babingo has suffered from a strange stomach ache since the choice of the ancestors fell on him."

"He can't therefore escape from his destiny. Whether he has been chosen by the spirits of ancestors, or he himself has chosen to be a healer, every novice must go through a long apprenticeship before acquiring knowledge. Also, it'll take not less than nine moons for Intu Ngolo Babingo to acquire the rudiments of healing science.

"The healing properties of a plant depend on the power of the deity to which it is linked. To succeed, the initiated healer must establish a close relationship with the corresponding deity linked to the plant in question."

On the first day of his initiation, Intu Ngolo Babingo was introduced into one of the three sacred forests by the great healer who knew all its nooks and crannies. Communication between the great healer and Intu Ngolo Babingo was rather tedious. Nga Mpandu barely spoke French. The apprentice healer therefore had to guess the meaning of the messages of his master. The Nuodu forest, a sort of mother earth, was for a long time a big reserve where one could find plenty of game, wood, precious metals, and medicinal plants capable of healing all sorts of illnesses.

"I'll require the permission of the powers in charge of this sanctuary to initiate you into the healing properties of the plants which heal the sicknesses that at times modern medicine is incapable of curing," the healer informed his new protégé.

"Under certain conditions and as you progress in your initiation, you'll be able to converse with sacred trees, in particular with the *Iroko* tree. After the observance of a certain ritual, it's in this great sacred tree in which we confide in order to be able to save a sick person who is under a spell or bewitched.

"The *Iroko* contributes to the treatment of so many illnesses that it would be tiresome to itemize them all for you. I will limit myself to citing some of them: against sorcery, miscarriage, madness, epilepsy, malaria, sexual weakness, snake bite, female infertility and so on. Very often, you'll need to intervene to save a member of the family or an inhabitant of the village by using the leaves, the bark, the roots, or yet still the chips of the *Iroko*. The remedy is obtained by different modes of operation which are maceration, decoction, infusion, or trituration.

"You must also know that, according to what one wants to use it for, the efficacy of the remedies depends on the observance of certain rituals such as the days or the hours favourable to the extraction of diverse components from the sacred tree. All that will require traditional knowledge that you'll need to acquire with time."

On his return from the visit to the first sacred forest, Intu Ngolo Babingo hurried to record in his note-book the rudiments of traditional medicine which the great healer had started to teach him. He realized that he would have quite a lot to do in order to completely enter into the secrets of the gods of the sacred forests. He realized also that on account of communication difficulties with the head of the lineage, his learning of the language was proving to be urgent.

For a very long time, the formal education of children in the village had remained an intractable problem for the authorities. Despite the repeated efforts of the traditional chief, awareness-driving campaigns, and sometimes threats by teachers, absenteeism, and most often, school dropout have marked the life of this village and that of the surrounding ones.

Clearly, the villagers thought that a system which did not take into account their peculiar circumstances and, above all, their vital existential needs was not meant for them. It is during the dry season and that of the light rain that a farmer needs most the help of the members of his family and more particularly that of children to plant cassava, potatoes, beans, or other food products. During the rainy seasons, when no activity was possible in open air, men, women, and children were available to carry out diverse transitional activities of their choice, without that upsetting the social equilibrium. Free from farm work, children could also go to school.

But the official school calendar seemed to be made for the inhabitants of urban areas and not for the rural folk who formed three quarters of the population of the country. In other climes, school calendars had been established by taking into consideration the needs of the entire community. When, against all odds, the children of rural areas who only spoke their mother tongue went to the official school of the village, they found themselves before a teacher who communicated with them in an opaque language supposed to be the one in which they should henceforth learn to read, write, and count. It was through extraordinary efforts of application and concentration that they were able to retain the scraps of knowledge which teachers strove to transmit to them.

Very often, children, who wrongfully thought that their presence in school served no good purpose, dropped out of school with the complicity of their parents.

Everyone was still surprised today that it was in the rural regions that the literacy rate was the lowest while at the same time, the number of school dropouts was largely above the national average. It would have been logical and definitely much more attractive to teach children many productive and very useful things if, during their first years, the school had provided them with knowledge in their mother tongue.

Mpiri was the only exception that proved the rule. Son of the district's road-surveyor, he was the only member of the lineage to have been to school up till the end of elementary school. Moreover, having been to the school of the head of lineage, he possessed cultural and linguistic knowledge which Intu Ngolo Babingo needed. He was therefore the guardian, the mentor, and interlocutor appointed for Intu Ngolo Babingo's apprenticeship.

Intu Ngolo Babingo had always known that language constituted an important component of his culture. But he was too far from imagining to which degree Téké language was strongly influenced by the philosophy, mode of thinking, and way of life of the village. He would later learn that a simple salutation should respond to a very precise ritual. For example, when a young person meets a person older than himself, he must be the first to greet by adding *a great brother* followed by a light but quite visible bending of the bust, as a sign of respect. This rule of decorum changes when a young person visits an older one. It is he who first greets his young visitor with warmth, to show his affection and hospitality.

Rather than make him repeat words and sentences, Mpiri endeavoured to transmit linguistic knowledge to Babingo through essential elements of culture, by choosing to leverage everyday life events. Mpiri handled this by creating opportunities for Babingo and him to meet.

"How would you handle greeting Nga Mpandu, the old soothsayer and healer?" Mpiri asked his student.

"As done during our first visit where nobody shook his hand, I'll say a simple good morning in the language."

"No," corrected Mpiri. "Nga Mpandu isn't only an old man to whom everybody owes respect by virtue of his age, but also because he's a great healer and a soothsayer. For that reason, he's always been held in veneration by all of us. Therefore to greet him, you'll need to revere him by stressing the honourable functions that he performs in our society."

"The last time that I accompanied him to Nuodu forest, he offered me barks of the *Iroko* to use as infusion to completely cure me of my dysentery. How should I thank him in our language?"

"If the expression 'thank you' does exist in our language, the Téké still resort indiscriminately to two expressions; either they praise the ancestors and God *"our ancestors have seen and accepted it"* or make a simple show of gratitude articulated by a *"long life to you."*

It is by very small clues that Mpiri put Babingo to the test during diverse conversational exercises starting from daily life events: the family, agricultural activities, hunting, the habitat, dress code, the weather, eating habits, professions, marriages and dowry, all served as pretext for motivating Babingo to immerse himself in the culture and subtleties of the Téké language.

Despite his application, Babingo had many problems familiarizing himself with intonations. For several months, Babingo tried to draw up rules with the view to standardizing a language which was not yet standardized. The Téké language spoken in Odiba village was only a variant of six others spoken in different parts of the country. Babingo carefully recorded his observations in notes each evening as soon as he retired into his hut. Drawing on his theoretical knowledge in linguistics, he undertook a comparative study – similarities and differences - with other languages. Structures of words, grammatical forms of all new expressions were examined; nothing was left to chance.

Babingo was eager to promote the development of a written and spoken Téké common to all the speakers of this language. He dreamt of seeing his maternal language, already spoken by one third of the inhabitants of his country, acquire the status of national language, like two or three others. To this end, Babingo had to ceaselessly learn in order to gain knowledge of the immense cultural richness and linguistic depth of the Téké people.

The sacred Albé forest is the place where, since the dawn of time, the spirits of kings and dignitaries of Odiba have been resting. To communicate with their ancestors, the descendants of royal families and only they, could have access to this forest where meetings for the initiated were organized.

Access to the forest was strictly forbidden to the female. However, paradox of paradoxes, the ceremonies were directed by a great octogenarian priestess, the guardian of the best kept secrets of the authorized lineages. The choice of the priestess owed nothing to chance. Apart from being the descendant of a king or a deceased high ranking dignitary, she had to undergo, for many years, the initiatory ordeals of the most rigorous nature, starting from the time her predecessor is still alive. Before her appointment, the sage in the village has to consult oracles to be sure that they are in favour of her enthronement.

It was into this sacred place that one day, Nga Mpandu, the great soothsayer, brought Babingo, the apprentice healer, at the beginning of his seventh month in Odiba village.

"Here," declared Nga Mpandu the healer, "the initiated were meeting on certain nights to communicate with royal ancestors. Whether it was about a dispute that they were unable to resolve or a calamity that they couldn't overcome, it was here they and the sages met, in a sort of retreat to invoke, supplicate, and sometimes conjure the spirits of late kings until a solution was found to the concerns of the living. Responses to their supplications could suddenly emerge during the nocturnal ceremony. They could also be transmitted one or several days later through dreams and which only the sages could decode or translate into comprehensible languages for common mortals. Each tree in the sacred forest has its double among the interred deceased royals and each one in this hallowed graveyard possesses curative properties."

"Is it possible to know the illnesses that one can still heal in our days by plucking the leaves or by extracting the bark of a particular tree?" Babingo dared to ask.

"This arboreal cemetery is under the protection of high dignitaries, descendants of royal ancestors. It's forbidden to touch one of these trees or to pluck a leave from it, remove a bark or all other extracts without authorisation. It's also necessary to know the specific incantations to which each tree of the forest responds for their extracts to provide the expected healing effect.

"For completely exceptional reasons, during rituals organized at the end of the heavy rainy season, the adult male population of the village and the surrounding villages can access the forest, to formulate wishes. Some expect to be healed of a disease declared incurable by modern medicine, others to touch a tree that has the power to arouse fertility in one of their wives. At the right time, with the agreement and benediction of dignitaries, I'll disclose to you the ingredients and other secrets to record in your notebook."

One evening, between two notes of vocabulary or linguistic terms, Babingo made time to write to Ingrid.

"Dear Ingrid,

You must be wondering if I'm still alive. Since the last letter which I addressed to you while I was still in Toulouse, I've failed to check on you and Kikimayô and above all, to inform you that I'm no longer in France.

It's unforgiveable of me, even if my unannounced departure was caused by a crucial reason.

Indeed, it'll soon be seven moons (seven months), as we say here, that I've been in Africa. I've taken the decision not just to leave France to return to my country, but

I've resolved to take a great bold step forward by making what can be called a complete and radical return to my roots.

Yes, I' in Odiba village, the place of origin of Mamakouta, my mother.

For what reasons did I take this apparent radical decision? How was I able to execute my plan?

First of all, for what reasons? There were two. After the FEANF Congress held in Paris at the end of last year all the leaders and other prominent members of FEANF were victims of terrible reprisals, often orchestrated by the political leaders of their own countries. These politicians could not tolerate the numerous resolutions and other forms of denunciation that the African students' movements published to condemn their political leanings.

Concerned about what Africa would become at the epochal moment of life-changing choices, we students militated for the immediate independence, total and real of our continent while some politicians at the head of our autonomous or supposedly independent nations accepted compromises that we deemed dangerous.

With the tacit complicity of the backrooms of the renamed Ministry of Colonies, the police started hounding all the national and regional leaders of the Federation of African students. They were subjected to intimidations of all sorts. Some, afraid of being expelled, left France to serve in two young Republics in Africa, Guinea and Mali. Others rather chose to continue their studies in Eastern or Northern European countries most of which were supportive of the aspirations of African countries fighting for their sovereignty.

Almost all my friends made the choice to leave Metropolitan France to avoid being brought back by force to their countries of origin where they risked being subjected to reprisals which would scar them forever or lead to their death.

I could have come to take "refuge" in Iceland, your country, where I've, from now on, a strong tie in the person of Kikimayô. Thanks to the link which unites us, I don't in the least doubt that I would have been welcome.

But as I'd quite luckily finished my higher studies, I preferred to take the plunge by daring to return to my origins.

I could have returned quietly to Pointe-Noire or even to Brazzaville.

After expressing his bad mood or even terrible anger characteristic of him, Papa Makouta would certainly have arranged with his former colleagues, now powerful political personalities, to find me a job in our young university or in a Ministry as technical adviser.

I chose to come here, to Odiba, and that's the second reason, both to recharge my batteries and overcome a frustration: that of not being able to speak, write or count correctly in what is supposed to be my mother tongue.

The village is the perfect place of initiation to true life. No one can claim to really know what the inhabitants of the rural communities of the numerous countries of our continent endure in terms of deprivations, nor appreciate their real needs, if he or she has never lived in this environment. Those who, by their exotic fantasy, claim that it's nice to live in the countryside should live there for some time to experience it.

Yet, it's in villages that tangible bursts of genuine solidarity and sharing manifest themselves. At Odiba, it's common to see a person undertake heavy tasks to relieve his neighbour. The same sharing of moments of joy and difficulties. The events which mark their daily life concern all the inhabitants of the village.

By choosing to come and live in the country and specifically in the village, I'd the objective of learning to speak the Téké language and if possible, promoting the standardization of the written form through the organization of its structures and grammatical rules.

And although the oracles have granted my request, they also added a condition to their acceptance.

I must not only be initiated into the ancestral culture of which the language is only one of the component parts, but be compulsorily subjected to the initiation into the science of healing. According to the spirits of the ancestors, I must be able to heal members of the lineage of possible illnesses, and especially be invested with the capacity to protect them against all manner of malevolence.

Irony of fate! I found myself obliged to oppose Papa Makouta who wanted me to study medicine at all cost. And now, the oracles have decided that I'll be soothsayer-healer, in other words, a doctor equipped with the power to heal visible and invisible illnesses!

For me to be initiated into this science considered to be the most prestigious of professions among the Téké, I've been entrusted to Nga Mpandu, the great soothsayer-healer of Odiba and surrounding villages. And for the nearly seven moons that I've been living here, I've been able to go to the most sacred and famous forests and also other places which abound in medicinal plants of diverse healing powers.

It's through culture and everyday life events that I'm learning the language. This is thanks to the wisdom of my cousin − I should say of my brother − Mpiri, because as members of the same age-group and lineage, we must regard ourselves as brothers.

Guided by the vital elements of Téké culture, Mpiri has instilled in me the subtleties of the language.

I've been applying myself to documenting in my voluminous notebook the knowledge which is imparted to me, starting from lexical items to the names of medicinal plants which have the potency to heal an impressive array of illnesses.

It's an understatement to say that being in the heartland of my country, I'm living an exceptional experience.

Tradition against modernity, will you say? Not an issue for it isn't contradictory to keep tradition perennially alive and at the same time move towards modernity. It's important that the changes made are those desired by the major stakeholders that is, by the people themselves, because the changes must help them to preserve their identity.

Be that as it may, I've found here the rationale for my cultural reintegration and drive for the achievement of my objective: the standardization of my language, and, at the right time, its promotion to the rank of national language among others.

Share my affectionate love and kisses with Kikimayô and your parents while keeping the lion's share for yourself."

Intu Ngolo Babingo

The heavy rainy season arrived with the slackening if not total paralysis of activities in the village. The rain is perceived among the Téké as a sign of the wrath of nature against man. It is certainly necessary for it to fall to ensure the fertility of the soil. But it is this same rain which curbs all outdoor activities. Nothing resists it for it devours everything on its wake.

When bad weather looms, people stop everything to take cover, while waiting for better days. This period was for Babingo the perfect moment to converse with the elderly head of lineage who had become very close with him since his arrival in the village. From him, he could deepen his knowledge, not only in the norms that govern communal life, but also in the acquisition of many proverbs, which provide the true lessons of indispensable wisdom conducive to harmonious coexistence. He could understand the imperious need of pooling the strengths of people belonging to the same community, especially the absolute duty of protection within the same lineage. He could now better appreciate the strong correlation between the idea of freedom and the preservation of order. The respect of traditions, harmony and intergenerational dialogue was rightly appropriated for what it was: the foundation of an indispensable cog for the preservation of authentic autochthonous cultures.

Whether it was about resolving inter-lineage conflicts, or conflicts between two individuals, the elders had the duty to provide proverbs which served as lesson of forgiveness that promote reconciliation between the parties involved. The stay-at-home type of life which the long rainy season imposed on him also allowed Babingo to put finishing touches to the writing of lexis in Téké and French languages. He also started to compose, little by little, some rudiments of a standardized language for the use of all speakers of Téké. It was necessary for him to model at all cost, all the characteristics of the language, from its grammatical structure up to the most complex terms. Phonology and more specifically classifications of consonants and vowels, syntax and wordings, nominal and verbal categories, in short, all the particularities of the language should be definitively codified to constitute the future standard.

Babingo dreamt of a learned society within which all the intellectual and material resources could be mobilized to foster the promotion of national languages in his country. While closely examining this idea, little did he know that he would face fierce opposition on the issue, particularly from the intellectual elite.

Beyond these dreams, he would always remember the terrible fright he had one morning, at the sight of what he first took to be a ghost before realizing that it was a being in flesh and blood, a living being whom he eventually recognized.

Chapter Fourteen

In one foggy morning on the onset of Harmattan, the inhabitants of Odiba experienced the strongest emotion ever known in the memory of "Odibians." It was first a noise coming from a faraway skyline, hardly audible, originating from the eastern part of the village. Then, as it increased progressively at the advance of the crowd, one could make out the voices of children stressing, like a slogan, the three syllables of a well-known word: 'mundele!', 'mundele!', 'mundele!'

The dense troop which surged towards old Makolondinga's compound seemed to be escorting a figure, a sort of phantom hardly inconceivable in this environment: a slender figure, that one surmises to be feminine and with a milky skin colour.

Babingo sighted the shadow from afar. Frightened, he swiftly turned around, increased his pace to hide in his hut, far away from the throng. He believed to have recognized Ingrid, whom he first took to be an erring spirit, or a ghost appearing in this environment where no one was expecting it. It was, however, not a ghost but Ingrid in flesh and blood who called Babingo, lifting up her hand high to signify that she was truly a living being.

"Babingo, don't you recognize me? Why are you running away from me?"

"Is it you, Ingrid?"

"It's me, Alex, sorry, Intu Ngolo Babingo."

"How did you get here and what have you come here for? Whom did you leave little Kikimayô with?"

A multitude of questions, more or less sensible, burst out from the mouth of Babingo, who still did not understand why this young and frail person from a country where everything was aseptically neat and tidy, would take the risk of venturing right into the heart of the equatorial forest. Abandoning the cozy life she was living in her native Iceland to come and live in a village where one had to sometimes make extraordinary efforts to obtain potable water. Coming to bury oneself in this environment where, in the evening, people still used the light from a storm lamp or a candle? That, in Babingo's opinion, was totally at variance with logic.

After allowing Babingo to blow off steam, Ingrid tried to justify her move starting from the story of her journey. First, she lost no time in reassuring him about little Kikimayô who, according to her, was growing up well in his milieu where he lived his life as a little Icelander. It was also true that Kikimayô was *mollycoddled* by his grand-parents who seemed very happy to have a grandson close to them – their little milk chocolate – as they loved to call him.

"If I arrived here without real great difficulty," continued the young woman, "it's because I had practically followed your own itinerary by reading the last letter in which you announced your new 'abode' to me. Of course, I didn't pass through Leopoldville.

"It's from Paris where, after obtaining a three-month entry visa to Congo, I boarded a plane for a direct flight to Brazzaville. From the airport, I joined a taxi to the car park that led to the administrative center of the region. From there, with the help of *banabanas,* as bus assistants are called, I was able to board a vehicle bound for a village whose name I've forgotten but is located on the river bank of Ndjiri. And presto I was at Odiba!

"What have I come to do here? Since our first meeting in Toulouse, I knew by intuition that I was going to live an uncommon adventure with you, wherever the place that destiny would lead us. After your departure from Reykjavik following your visit on the occasion of

Kikimayô's birth, I registered for an evening course to study cultural anthropology and, especially Bantu culture and philosophy.

"Without in any way claiming to have understood everything, I believe I understand that Bantu wisdom valorizes and stresses the hierarchy of powers, specifically those which brought me here to you. By coming to join you in Mamakouta's village, I knew that I hadn't made the choice for an easy life. I was aware that I wouldn't find Iceland's comfort which I was used to, here. I've chosen to live the same experience as you, while admitting that I can never have the same experience as you."

Ingrid truly and seamlessly shared the village life, practically under the same conditions with other women of old Makolondinga's compound.

The fetching of water was a chore they performed daily at the riverside, the priceless liquid that is boiled on a hearth made of earthenware to make it potable. Ingrid seemed to willingly submit to the rhythm of women's life in this village in the depths of Africa. She also participated in the gathering of cassava during harvest. The local culinary art had no secret for her. Squash sauce, meat of *ka*, *antelope*, partridge and other poultry, locusts and caterpillars made up her meals which she shared every evening with the members of the big family according to Téké custom.

Ingrid puzzled and at the same time irritated the inhabitants of the village, more particularly the women, most of whom were suspicious of her. The great priestess Ibitangu who supervised the cult of the sacred Eriti forest was not left out. She kept an eye on her through her disciples. Ingrid's smallest gestures and movements were reported to her. Now, the foreigner was curious about everything, wanted to know everything, see everything, do everything. People had even caught her in the act of roaming around the sanctuary.

Within a short time, she was able to have sustained conversation with the mothers of the village who ended up adopting her. The legendary Téké hospitality prevailed over suspicions. It had been reported to Ibitangu that Ingrid wanted to be initiated. Intrigued and charmed at the same time, the great priestess summoned her and informed her of her inability to submit to the sacrifices associated with entry into the sacred apprenticeship and the observance of the rules governing the life of an initiate.

Ingrid, who absolutely wanted to become an initiate of the Eriti cult had no fear of complying with all the rules and deserting her partner, Intu Ngolo Babingo, to go and spend the period of her religious apprenticeship for many months in the sanctuary. The taboos and secret rites should not be revealed to the non-initiated. Therefore, on her exit from the sacred forest, the seat of Eriti cult, her meeting with the deities as well as the secrets which she had been taught had to remain absolutely protected. She was, however, authorized to refer to the animal and plant worlds which formed, long before then, a typical vast ecological space in which she lived. This consecrated training school became, as a result of Ingrid's experience, not only a place of life but also a sanctuary where the silence of the forest encouraged meditation.

Thenceforth, the initiated Ingrid had to bear her "religious" name, testify to her membership of a totemic clan, and move about in the village in light sandals regardless of the season and the weather. She was also to leave the top of her body completely nude. Only her breasts were protected by a pure white wrapper in which she was covered to the tip of her feet. Ingrid returned to the secular world, completely transformed. If the entry into the "convent" responded to a quest for spirituality, Ingrid seemed to have made discoveries that were beyond her wildest imagination.

By her own admission, she had rediscovered herself. From then on, she, compared to her partner, Babingo, became stricter in her everyday demeanour, indeed more respectful of traditions, prohibitions and taboos. The exotic village life that both led seemed to go on without any incident. Babingo advanced in his linguistics and healing studies.

However, Ingrid and her partner never foresaw the extraordinary event that would hasten their departure from Odiba.

Chapter Fifteen

Alerted by whatever rumour mill, Mpiri suddenly emerged from the forest. Sputtering, he took the footpath leading to the compound, to announce the news to Babingo and Ingrid.

"There is a threat of war at Nkuna, sorry in Brazzaville," he shouted entering precipitately into the hut where the couple was resting.

"Don't talk about war," Babingo replied. "You surely want to say there is a rumor of a revolt or of a revolution there?"

Mpiri explained in his own way that there were tensions in the capital between the Head of State and the people. Possibly even the beginning of an uprising organized by the militants of the trade union. With the rumor becoming more insistent, Babingo and Ingrid decided to go to Nkuna, alias Brazzaville, to find out for themselves what was really happening there.

Thus it was that soon afterwards, they found themselves searching for an unlikely means of transport to take them to the capital city, their luggage made up of only a few personal belongings. They got into the first canoe which took them to other side of the river, on dry land. The wait by the side of the road was endless.

Very luckily, the lorry which operated weekly between the capital and the villages of the district was, that very day, passing through Bamona. After some minutes of negotiation and the promise of *matabiche*, the driver agreed to place Ingrid in the cab beside him, while Babingo had to make do with one of the seats fixed in the lorry in open air. He had for company not just other passengers but also baskets of smoked fish, crates of fruits and vegetables.

After some hours of travel on chaotic tracks and roads, the lorry arrived at the outskirts of Brazzaville at night. The faces and clothes of the passengers were red and dusty.

At the entrance to the capital city, the driver was stopped by a patrol of soldiers who were not just armed to the teeth but were also particularly ill-tempered.

"Where are you coming from and why do you want to enter the city at this ungodly hour?" the one who appeared to lead the patrol asked in local language.

And, without waiting for a response to his question, he ordered all the passengers out of the lorry. He subjected men, women, and children to a series of very thorough search. Babingo and his partner realized then, not without surprise, that they had arrived in a city under siege.

The lorry driver had the intelligence to avoid the main roads where the patrols were stationed. By dint of juggling, he succeeded in driving his passengers and goods to the closest motor park. Everywhere was deserted and in a disquieting calm. Intu Ngolo Babingo and Ingrid went through unimaginable ordeals crossing the many check points dotted on all the main roads leading to their destination.

They eventually landed at Poto-Poto, in the house of cousin Itoua, a policeman by profession, in the hope of finding there the needed tranquility amidst the prevailing uproar.

At Poto-Poto, at the end of Voula Street, in the residential area of Plateau de 15 ans was a small but charming colonial-style bungalow. The house was conspicuous by its tile-covered roof, yellow-painted walls as well as doors and windows painted in green.

Papa Makouta retired into this residence, with his wife, as soon as he had been able to assert his right to a comfortable retirement package, as a high-ranking civil servant of Overseas France. A day following his arrival in Brazzaville, Babingo, flanked by Ingrid, went to pay a visit to his parents, in this new residence which they had just heard about. The surprise visit of the lost child whose presence in Odiba they had got wind of, was both a source of joy and palpable friction.

Here was a son for whom Makouta had nourished so much ambition, in whom he had seen the first medical doctor of the clan, for whom he had predicted a future political career of the highest order and a marriage with a girl from his own ethnic group. Not satisfied with hunkering down in the village in search of some illusive linguistic discoveries, here he comes now with a foreigner, without warning!

The big surprise—and a pleasant one at that--was when Babingo, in attempting to explain the reason for his choice, expressed himself in perfect Téké, and went to great lengths to avoid code-switching, mixing his speech with a foreign language. He boasted to his father about all the richness of their culture and of their language, as well as the healing properties of the plants that abounded in their locality.

The element of surprise over, Makouta observed with pride that his son had so much immersed himself in Téké culture and had acquired from there a knowledge and a know-how that many people of his generation would certainly envy him for. However, Makouta could not stomach the unpalatable truth that his son had chosen a partner who was not from his ethnic group. He obstinately defended the principle that each one should preserve his culture, that extra-ethnic and extra-racial marriages were an obstacle to the preservation of each one's culture and worldview.

As usual, Mama Makouta had no voice in the matter. Hardly was she able to ask after Kikimayô. Although Babingo tried to convince his father about his error in respect of the exaggerated sense of ethnicity, the paterfamilias would not budge. The conversation, in Téké, was very heated throughout the visit.

Mama Makouta managed to ease the atmosphere by offering a succulent meal of antelope meat and squash sauce, with pieces of very fresh cassava as accompaniment. The subsequent meetings between Babingo and his father would most likely be very stormy as well, but during this meal enjoyed by all, the atmosphere was calm.

The following day, two days before the national independence celebrations of the country, Babingo and Ingrid decided to go on a tour of the city. Their movement was held in check by multitude of workers who, defying the policemen present, surged forward towards the square of the central railway station. As the day progressed, the crowd swelled up; those arriving from Bacongo joined the Poto-Poto group, which had pitched camp there since dawn.

Babingo and Ingrid unwillingly found themselves witnesses of an event of rare intensity, during which the main actors seemed to be spoiling for a fight. Conspicuous among the many demonstrators were workers by reason of their sheer numbers and also their distinctive garb. Also present were civil servants and employees of private companies. The ringleaders harangued the crowd, peppering their speeches with hostile words against the authorities.

When two trade union leaders appeared at the square, the crowd welcomed them with deafening applause before listening to them. In fact, they were two leaders known for their radical anti-Establishment postures. One of them hoisted himself onto a nearby barrel turned upside down to give a speech far remote from the issue of wage demands. The political underpinnings of the protest were self-evident.

Hemmed in by a patrol of policemen armed with truncheons, the demonstrators could not carry out their plan of holding a meeting at the trade union center. They decided therefore to march to the seat of government.

But, as one should expect, the movement was stopped outright by the police visibly determined to nip every attempt at rioting in the bud. The protesters stretched out into small groups, taking different routes to evade the vigilance of the police.

It was then that Babingo, who, together with Ingrid, was attempting to follow the multitude as a rather discrete spectator, met someone unexpectedly, in this environment where tension was more than palpable.

In the crowd which, after foiling the tactics of the police, had improvised a meeting at the city council square, Babingo caught sight of a figure which except for her age, reminded him of Tessa, his childhood friend. He discretely went closer to the female protester, not without hesitation, given her mature and commanding carriage. He went closer to her again and paused again. The more he went closer to the unknown woman, the more the traits of the woman gave him cause to believe that he was in the presence of the person whom he thought the figure to be. Tessa, his friend in Pointe-Noire, the one who, for the first time, had motivated him to speak a language of the country. And this, contrary to the order he had received from his father! But perhaps it was her look-alike, so he still hesitated. Finally he took his courage into his hands and dared to call the unknown woman.

"You so much resemble a childhood friend of mine. Could you be Tessa?"

Hardly had Babingo finished pronouncing the two syllables than the unknown woman of a few seconds ago jump at his neck, shouting "Alex!", screaming an exclamation which attracted the attention of the demonstrators around them. The two childhood friends took cognizance of the time that had flown by. Their glances met, in a conspiratorial silence that conveyed a sort of eternal regret; that of not being able to develop together because of ethnic conservatism.

"When did you come back from Metropolitan France and what are you doing here?"

"I came back some months ago but I went directly to Odiba, my mother's village."

"Please, meet Ingrid, my partner, who has had the courage or the thoughtlessness of following me to the heart of the village.

"So you, Tessa, what became of you and what are you also doing here in the midst of demonstrators?"

"At the end of my primary school studies, I was admitted to a girls' school. While pursuing my high school studies, a great tragedy struck. My father, the only support for the family, died abruptly. In high school, I was among the best pupils, and I was considered brilliant by our teachers. I was obtaining excellent marks in both Science and Arts subjects.

"Then Dad, an interpreter at the trial court of Pointe-Noire was struck down by a ferocious coronary attack in front of a full audience. He was interpreting into local language an apparently ominous verdict which the judge of the court was giving. The State Prosecutor had requested the death penalty for a defendant who had murdered a young woman, after raping her. Was it possible that my father had such strong emotions about the case that he died of it?

"According to eye-witnesses, my father had benefitted from a swift medical intervention. An emergency doctor dispatched by the general hospital arrived in an ambulance which entered the law court in whirlwind fashion. Despite the wonderful efforts made by the doctor, the worst occurred. My poor dad had given up the ghost even before arriving at the general hospital. At the age of forty-five, he was still in the prime of life. As an accomplished athlete, he had represented the country in various competitions. His death was for us a real financial and emotional blow.

"Since according to our beliefs, no one dies naturally, my paternal family accused my maternal grandmother of witchcraft. She allegedly caused the death of my father so that all his possessions would revert to her clan. It was a pretext to snatch from us the house which my parents had just bought in the classy neighbourhood and into which we had just moved.

"As fate would have it, the small bungalow acquired through a home loan was still under mortgage. The malevolent people would have been obliged to repay the debt over a period of twenty-five years. Given their joblessness and general impoverishment, none of them had the means of doing that. We also didn't have it, but thanks to the life insurance coverage to which Dad had subscribed as a member of the Judicial Assistants' Credit Union, we were able to keep the house without, however, being totally freed from the crippling debt.

"My mother's petty trading as a smoked fish retailer was hardly enough to defray the expenses related to the school fees for my brother and me. For this reason, I found myself obliged to cut short my high school education in order to enter the newly established School of Social Work. Thanks to my civil servant salary, I've been able, since the very first year of employment, to send monthly remittance to my mother to alleviate her financial burden.

"Some years later, I met a man of the same ethnic group as myself whom I married. A railway worker who became a labour union leader. It was he who, some minutes ago, stood on a barrel haranguing the crowd, at the Railway Station Square. It is him you now see over there, with a loud speaker in his left hand, surrounded by other protesters, in full discussion with a representative of the mayor. His name is Okima Maurice."

"Tessa, I'm puzzled and would like to know the true motives of the insurgents. For, since this morning, I haven't been able to establish any demand with the least claim to salary adjustment or social improvement. Could this be about an uprising that is basically political in nature?"

"Only Maurice will be able to answer your question, at the right time, that is after the protesters have left the public places they have besieged. Unfortunately I don't have the sense that it'll be over soon, given the overcharged nature of the protest. I even doubt if the representative of the city council can bring an end to the agitations.

"By the way, I advise you to take Ingrid away from here, for, on account of the prevailing tension, her presence, even if discreet among the protesters, may be misconstrued and misperceived."

It was in a café located in the middle of the avenue leading to the city council that Okima Maurice met Babingo. The charismatic trade unionist seemed worried because his comrades who, very early in the morning, had succeeded in besieging the gate of the Presidential Palace saw themselves confronting a military cordon of a foreign army based in a neighbouring country, invited to help to protect the palace. He was concerned that the protest would go beyond what the union intended and degenerate into an uncontrollable riot.

"It seems you want to understand the motives at the root of our protest and our popular outrage," Maurice asked Babingo without ceremony.

"Yes, Maurice, because in my opinion, your protest should be about salary demands. I believe there are established avenues for discussing and resolving such issues with the authorities. Unless of course, you've reached the point of no-return which would justify recourse to the type of confrontation we're witnessing now."

"The differences between the government and the trade unions are profound. Because of the economic crunch the country is experiencing, the government wants to cancel the labour-related gains made over the years after a difficult struggle by public servants. But then the State, which should lead by example is always wasting public funds. Politicians, ministers and parliamentarians are notorious for their obscene display of opulence.

"Strengthened by his recent electoral victory, the Head of State wanted to consolidate his power by merging the different political parties into a single party. He wanted to do the same by creating a single trade union, in plain disregard for our opinion. The mass movements which we, unionists represented, had suggested the creation of a single political party under two conditions, the first demand being the reduction of the number of ministers and deputy ministers from eighteen to eight in total. The second demand concerned our opposition to the creation of a single political party and of a single labour union which we consider to be an instrument of domination and oppression. Instead of a single party, we preferred the establishment of a confederation of parties

where all political leanings would have the right
to freely express themselves. We wanted for our
country, the establishment of an African socialist and pluralistic society.

"Faced with the Head of State's intransi-
gence, we, labour union representatives, were
left with no choice than to boycott the Commission charged with the setting up of the structures of the one-party system by giving out a
strike notice for the 13th of August.

"In response to what is just a strike notice,
the government had, already on the eve, sent
the police to arrest and detain our two comrades who were at the Trade Union center
to prepare for the demonstration planned for
the next day. It is this arbitrary arrest that has
added fuel to the flames. Do you know that the
masses of workers and numerous sympathizers
went this morning to force open the door of
the prison to set free the unjustly imprisoned
labour unionists? That's not the end. We'll fight

on relentlessly and will do all we can to force this corrupt government to relinquish power."

"How are you people going to do that? It seems that a detachment of a foreign army, made up of several hundreds of soldiers, has surrounded the presidential palace. No group of protesters will be able to cross the security barricade installed at the entrance of the palace."

"The people's determination will triumph over all intimidations, wherever they may come from. We harbour no resentment either against the country of origin of this army or against its citizens who have settled here, but we won't accept that they interfere in our internal problems. Now that you're well-informed of the reasons for our conflict with the government and the justness of our struggle, let me go and join my comrades in front of the palace."

Babingo, who seemed to have been convinced by his arguments, followed the labour leader. Both of them joined the protesters.

While various groups of protesters assembled in front of the presidential palace, the labour unionists tried to avoid confrontations with the troops of the foreign army whose mission was to defend the building and its occupants. The soldiers stationed at the gate of the palace appeared as if on a war footing. The tactics of the labour union representatives then was to appeal to the moral and religious leaders of the country, as well as the representatives of other zones of influence for them to restrain the ardour of the soldiers that had come as reinforcement to save the government. A lost cause as the first reactions of stakeholders were rather timid.

Then there was an impasse, for the authorities thinking that the situation was under control as a result of the foreign support it had received, hardened its stance and promised to reinstall order, at whatever the price. Apprehension spread amongst the trade union circles as they tried in vain to contact the officer-in-charge of the foreign army.

The first dramatic turn of events came from the presidential palace.

Under pressure from the mob, President Kamanga accepted, not only to form a new government of reconciliation, but to also to postpone the plan of establishing a one-party system. All these last-minute commitments, unfortunately, did not convince the labour leaders and the young officers of the national army. They blamed the Head of State for having surrounded himself with arrogant and corrupt politicians, known for their ostentatious lifestyles.

The slogan for the rally was becoming more and more insistent. "Everybody to Mongali Roundabout". The protesters of the first days who, at dawn, were already at this iconic place had been joined by the leaders of youth organizations, their sympathizers, and students. The disapproval was unanimous. And like a tsunami, the protesters, surging from all zones, converged near the palace: a silent and well-disciplined throng made up of men, women, young boys and girls, who appeared astonishingly resolute.

The foreign troops, armed to the teeth and the national police which had taken position at the gate of the barricaded and impregnable palace, waited staunchly. The protesters, whose numbers were swelling by the minute, shouted hostile slogans at the President: "Kamanga: resign, Kamanga, resign!" But none could cross the gate of this fiercely guarded palace.

It was then that by a stroke of genius Okima Maurice, Tessa's unionist husband, decided to alert an influential figure in the country who had access to General Durand Dupré, the superior officer who was in command of the foreign army, to intervene. Against all expectations, the commander of this so much dreaded army agreed to meet the unionists.

Surprised by the unexpected success of Okima's move, a bit suspicious but relieved, the trade union leaders went to meet the foreign general. Strange discussions took place between personalities of dissimilar profiles. They alternated between hardly veiled threats and conciliatory words. The unionists succeeded in convincing the officer in the end that the causes being defended by the insurgents were just; they arose from a deep political crisis which could not be resolved by force.

During the meeting with the officer, the beginning of which was very stormy, the message the insurgents communicated was clear: the dispute that caused their disagreement with the government in place being internal by nature, did not at all warrant external intervention.

"Protecting a single man – even if a Head of State -, against a people is tantamount to scoffing the aspirations of these people," the union leader had declared.

The general hesitated a moment before taking the decision to refer the case to the military hierarchy and probably the political hierarchy of his country, far, very far away from the *theatre of operations.* After extensive explanations and prevarication, the long-awaited decision was made. Non-intervention was granted and the foreign troops received the order to depart from the presidential palace.

Then, the events followed one another at a breathtaking space. Two officers from the national army, Captain Mananga and Captain Dibomba, accompanied by trade unionists Ovelo and Mivindo entered the palace unannounced and with no regard for formalities, ordered President Kamanga to resign.

Thinking he still enjoyed the support of the foreign power, the Head of State refused, arguing that he was the only one that enjoyed legitimacy from the people. But, unfortunately for him, despite his insistent demand, he was eventually notified of the definitive refusal of the faraway "decision makers" to intervene.

President Kamanga had to be stripped of all the multifarious mandates which he had been holding concurrently. The man was indeed at once President of the Republic, Chairman of the Party, MP, and Mayor of the capital city.

From prevarications to last-minute shows of bravado, Kamanga, when finally informed of the nonintervention of the protecting external power, agreed to sign a resignation letter. Flooded by emotions this man, hitherto so powerful, suddenly realized that power had been decisively seized from his hands. In desperation, the soon-to-be ex-President wanted to negotiate his surrender. He started a pathetic dialogue with the officer who was holding his resignation letter.

"What fate do you have in store for me now? My wife and other members of my family, will they be spared? I demand that a country of exile be found for me."

Then, on further reflection, he stated that he wanted to join his wife abroad, in a city of his choice, mumbling that he was at a loss as to his next move.

"No harm will befall you if you comply with the directives which will be given to you, Officer Mananga replied him. "In your situation, it would be hazardous and especially dangerous for your life to let you leave the country. Because anything that would happen to you outside of here could be attributed to the invisible hands of the new authorities."

President Kamanga's dream metamorphosed for good into a nightmare when the young officers, spearheads of the insurrection, notified him of his arrest and his transfer to a prison of maximum security.

Thus ended the political career of a man who believed in the praises and other eulogistic words with which adulators covered him when he was at the peak of his glory.

Chapter Sixteen

When on the national radio, the mouthpiece of the new government who was reading a communiqué announced his name among other personalities invited to occupy ministerial positions, Babingo first thought it was a hoax. Then, he believed he had a daydream.

Thrown into a panic, he ran to look for Ingrid to tell her all the evil he thought about the person who had proposed his name, swearing in the name of all the gods that he would refuse his nomination. He was about to call Tessa when the latter reached him by telephone and showered him with kind congratulatory words.

"No and no, don't congratulate me, because I am not at all interested in this post. I don't in the least feel attracted to a political office. Can you tell me why Maurice screwed me up in this galley?"

"The best way to find out if Maurice was the initiator or not of your nomination would be that you ask him yourself. However, on my part, I believe I can find one or two reasons for your nomination. The trade unionists, leaders of the insurrection movement, have refused to be part of the governing team. The young officers who supported the protest have also chosen to return to the military camp. They've decided to entrust the reins of power of the country to civilians, preferably to technocrats.

"Many figures connected directly or indirectly to the team about to take over the political management of the country are your old FEANF comrades. In short, during the three days, you were seen in the multitude of protesters even if you'd discreetly avoided to be in the forefront. People identify you with the sympathizers. From there, to see you as a militant committed to the cause of the insurgents, was only a step quickly taken by the agitators now in power. If Maurice had perhaps given assurances concerning you to the Selection Committee for 'potential ministers,' it was surely not only him who thought about you."

"I don't in the least have the calling to be a politician. Straightaway, I am going to communicate my refusal to the new President, whose name I heard pronounced for the first time this morning when the spokesperson was reading the famous communiqué. What's his name again?"

"His name is Matoungoulou Dieudonné, specified Tessa his friend, adding: "rejecting your nomination would be considered an anti-patriotic act at a moment when the new administration is viewed by some as a government of novices. With the exception of the Head of State, none of the members is a politician;

they're all high level technocrats in their areas of specialisation. They're coming to remedy the catastrophic socio-economic situation of the country and will leave when things get better.

"Besides, if I remember well the names of the ministers, their deputies and the portfolios assigned to them, you'll be in charge of culture and literacy. Would that not be for you the opportunity you've long dreamt of to contribute your quota to this domain, which happens to be your area of specialization?"

The sub-ministry for Culture and Literacy of which Babingo will be in charge, had been placed under the umbrella of a gigantesque Ministry, equally in charge of Health, Labour, Education, Youth, and Sports. Sensitive to Tessa's arguments, Babingo changed his mind, consoled himself by thinking that his position as the one in charge of culture would offer him the chance of fulfilling his dream: the passing of a bill on major reform that will eventually render access to education in national languages mandatory. For sure, Babingo was aware that for success to crown such an effort, he would need to convince the members of government of the importance of this radical change of orientation in the educational system. However, he thought that since other African countries had succeeded in this effort, there was no reason why his country would not be able to effect this change. Therefore, it was at his very first meeting with the super Minister Balossa, that Babingo, arming himself with perfectly solid arguments that he believed were sufficiently convincing, decided to speak about his plan to his immediate boss.

"Comrade Minister, the culture which I'm in charge of within your vast department covers many domains ranging from the preservation of the national heritage to theater and cinematographic production, not forgetting deconsecrated cemeteries which have been converted into museums.

"Literacy is as much about children of pre-school age as it is about adults who have never been to school and who are legion in our villages and even in our towns. Now, it seems to me that we will not succeed in re-appropriating our culture unless we make it possible for a larger number of our people to have access to knowledge. That will only be possible if the masses of our compatriots understand what they're supposed to learn in order to build a future worthy of this name, each one according to their capacities.

"We can't expect our children to perform better in school, no matter what their social conditions are, unless they're taught in the languages they speak in their natural milieu. I therefore have the intention of proposing for your kind attention, a sufficiently documented text which, hopefully, should be adopted by the government in order that at the primary level, classes will be taught in national languages.

"I'm aware of the numerous obstacles that have to be surmounted. However, it's high time we appropriated for ourselves the real essence of our culture, namely, our way of thinking and expression."

"I understand you perfectly, dear comrade Intu Ngolo Babingo, but don't forget that we're a government of trailblazers and moreover a provisional administration, whose remit consists, as a matter of urgency, in sorting out the economy of the country by remedying all the social problems that occasioned the insurrection. We'll have a lot to do to accomplish the mission that has been assigned to us.

"I must also remind you, comrade Intu Ngolo Babingo, that we've an official language which is used for communication between compatriots from the north to the south and from the east to the west. As this language does not belong to any ethnic group, we've been able up till now to insulate the country from deleterious effects of ethnic identity in this regard.

Again, with the country having more than sixty vernaculars, which of them should be adopted as national languages? Believe me, no government will risk opening this Pandora box."

"Certainly, the socio-economic situation of the country obliges the government to devote itself to this as a topmost priority. But as unbearable as it is, this situation, I expect, is short-term. Learning in a language that one understands will ultimately liberate our people from the mediocrity that breeds endemic poverty. It isn't at all a question of changing the official language although this foreign language which is French cannot claim any positive connection with our innermost being, serving as it does to maintain our colonial past and to keep us there. But, I agree, this past is a part of our history.

"Our children would continue to learn the official language. It would be important to establish adult literacy and academic programmes in three to five languages chosen from the major languages of the country."

"I'm very sure that the speakers of the numerous other vernaculars which won't be retained will take exception to the domination of those which will have been promoted into national languages. It's equally important to thoroughly reform the entire educational system of the country, train teachers, and invest in new equipment. This becomes a daunting task since we haven't even as yet succeeded in building sufficient classrooms nor in equipping them. There are educational priorities other than the introduction of national languages in the educational system, my dear Babingo."

"Comrade Minister, you've just uttered the word: investment! Exactly, it's important to invest in the future of our children. Now, the numerous notorious failures in the rural areas lead to frustrations which will become more and more unbearable for our compatriots."

"Those are obsessions and imaginary fears invented by you and your ilk, utopian intellectuals, to impose your ideology which is totally at variance with scientific socialism. It's better to be pragmatic. That way, you avoid being discarded by history. Have you asked yourself if the rural people want their children to be educated in the official language or in what you pompously call national languages? And what if these people labelled the educational system, that you are recommending, cheap-rate teaching?"

"It'll be important to establish a bilingual system or even multilingual system of education within which the official language will have its place.

"Comrade Balossa, permit me to add very respectfully, with regard to doctrine, that it was the utopian socialists who, in a certain region of the world that we know very well, fought to introduce paid holidays, reduction of working hours, forty-hour week, while the scientific socialists were busy inventing many things, including gigantic political prisons and other systems of tyranny.

"Therefore, no polemic, please, on the virtues or misdeeds of socialist orientations. I just wish that our discussions allowed us to delve into the issue of the recovery of our culture and worldview, of which language re-appropriation constitutes one of the key components."

Having run out of arguments but determined to nip in the bud what he considered Babingo's stupid idea, super minister Balossa eventually tasked him to submit a detailed position paper on his project. After which an intra-ministerial Commission would examine, if necessary, the strange proposals of his deputy.

If you want to kill a proposal which disturbs you, create a committee and charge it to study it!

Balossa instituted a committee and asked Babingo to chair it. Naturally, it was called the Babingo Committee.

Chapter Seventeen

It is an understatement to say that Babingo was proud to have succeeded in overcoming the reservations of his comrade, the super Minister Balossa. Real joy could be read on his face. It was therefore with overwhelming enthusiasm that he acted to assemble, at a very short notice, specialists of various degrees of teaching. There were also in this gigantic committee, luminaries from diverse fields: linguistics, psychology, sociology, and numerous other professional bodies. He equally made sure to include leaders of associations of students' parents operating throughout the country.

And, like a candidate hungry for the approbation of voters, Babingo endeavoured to outline the virtues of the system he was championing, not hesitating to label as aberrant the continuation of any policy that no longer responded to the needs of a nation which was attempting to restore its cultural identity. He expounded his vision for the new school whose overarching objective was the introduction of national languages in the educational system.

The august assembly of committee members seemed to listen to Babingo with such rapt attention that one could easily believe that the members would have wished to see a similar reform introduced much earlier. They appeared to have found a leader capable of helping them to realize this dream.

Babingo seized the opportunity to insist on the necessity to, as quickly as possible, grow out of the prevailing national humiliation with which the country seemed to be satisfied. "Can there be real independence if one continues to think and express oneself through a language different from that of one's natural environment? There is urgent and I count on you to ensure that our country becomes one of the first promoters of change in this area," stressed Babingo.

The different aspects entailed in the terms of reference were entrusted to sub-committees, charged to develop innovative proposals for submission to the State.

These included a sub-committee on linguistics, a sub-committee responsible for the identification of the vernaculars eligible for promotion to the rank of national languages on the basis of well-defined criteria, a sub-committee in charge of the training of teachers, and another whose role would be to go to the field to evaluate the needs of the people throughout the entire territory. Lastly, the nature and quantity of indispensable teaching materials was a task assigned to another subcommittee.

To his great surprise, Babingo discovered that the support of the first days was only a pretense. Contrary to his expectation, the enthusiasm quickly gave way to a barrage of questions which betrayed reservation and more often avowed opposition.

"How can we re-appraise the unitary conceptualization of the nation and play down the ethnic differences which characterize the relationships among the peoples of this country?" asked Bassila, one of the most influential committee members? The diversity of languages of communication between our ethnic groups is an accepted fact. It is unclear if the introduction of national languages is part of the first concerns of the people.

"One would be wrong to underestimate the linguistic irredentism of the rural peoples and especially of intellectuals. The love for the mother tongue is a strongly anchored sentiment," Bassila concluded.

Bamoutou, a committee member from the association of students' parents, went further by emphasizing that the speakers of minority languages will not easily accept the decision of choosing national languages of teaching outside of theirs, because of what they consider to be their affection for their language, their feeling of belongingness and their ethnic identity.

Boboloko, another committee member well known in the intellectual circles, emphasized the reasons for the people's strong attachment to the French language. It also enhances their social status. Because of its status as the official language, the French language is ever-present in all places and domains. It remains the major driver of social elevation.

The wise Matindou, the self-taught philosopher, unanimously respected for his scholarship, brought up his own evidence to support Babingo's project.

"When, at age nine thereabout, the divisional commander of the colonial era forced my father to send me to school as he had done for the other children of the village, we were all, with the exception of the schoolteacher's son, unable to understand a single word of what the school master was saying to us. For many months, we had to make superhuman efforts to guess, and if possible, understand the meaning of words. A feeling of frustration was widely shared by us all.

"Acquisition of knowledge was done through forced march, only in the French language, which was very different from the language that we spoke at home. Because one only learns very well when one understands, we lagged behind with many handicaps all along our schooling. Our Class Six teacher had difficulty properly preparing us for the primary school certificate examinations. The results were poor. I was lucky to be among the survivors of the shipwreck, of that calamity. In our class, the dropouts were legion.

"I'm convinced that the results would have been better if there had been a link with the teaching imparted within the context of our life and our environment.

"On a personal level, after decades of frustration, I was able to learn to read and write in what is supposed to be my mother tongue and which I was strictly forbidden to speak in school, at the risk of punishment."

Tessa, who was also participating in the deliberations of the Committee in her capacity as representative of social workers argued further.

"In my former position as social worker, I kept very close contact with families of modest means, as much in the urban areas as in the rural areas. I was able to observe that, without exception, the members of these social classes could not monitor the performances of their children for the simple reason that they themselves did not speak the French language. It's high time that children, all the children, accessed knowledge through their mother tongues or at the very least through one of the major national language families. The task will not be easy. However, this is the time to act, if we want all our children to acquire knowledge through their own culture and not by relying on borrowed exogenous know-how."

Dispassionately, Babingo took note of the reservations and skepticisms, as well as the approvals. While there had been no sustained opposition, contributions of committee members that were unequivocally favourable were not many. And, by their passiveness, the silent majority was able to create the impression that it was not against the wonderful reform proposed by Babingo. It was true that under the circumstances, few people dared show their stand. Caution had to be exercised in order not to ruffle the feelings of Babingo, the Deputy Minister who was moreover the Chairman of the Committee. Hypocrisy was, sometimes, necessary.

The reservations of some and the silence of others enlightened Babingo and allowed him to note the pitfalls to avoid in order to guarantee the chances of the success of this audacious reform that the introduction of national languages in the educational system entailed.

Far from allowing himself to be disheartened, Babingo picked up his arguments again, now well grounded, to sway the most reluctant of the committee members to his side.

He started,

"We're going to start work. The subcommittees will each, according to its area of specialization and capacity, have to propose solutions to overcome the obstacles which I've heard mentioned, at various levels.

"It'll be necessary to identify the three or five national languages to retain, using objective criteria. The yardsticks should include the numerical size of speakers, regional representativeness of the languages chosen and the significance of research works already undertaken on them with respect to the level of standardization, analysis of grammatical system and other findings likely to facilitate their learning.

"We must assess teachers' training needs as well as the type of complementary teaching resources needed. Human and financial efforts will be required. But whatever the importance of sacrifice in these domains, the government should appreciate the fact that these are investments that aim at securing a weal, a better life for future generations. Besides, the costs involved are much lower than the enormous military expenditure that our country has been incurring for many years to protect itself against an imaginary enemy.

"This isn't about throwing overboard the official language, so hallowed by the Constitution, but to place it on the same pedagogical footing as the languages being promoted.

"We must put an end to the mindset that our national languages are incapable of transmitting scientific knowledge. Countless are the examples that prove the contrary. Valorizing our national languages means securing the cultural identity of our children, before it's too late. Because the child that cannot use his or her regular familiar parlance is incapable of exteriorizing, of expressing his or her feelings and interests.

"At all the stages of our research, we must, through representative bodies, consult and inform the people, in order to reassure them and convince ourselves of the merit of our choices.

"Know that we can only properly conceive of the world if we appropriate our culture. Language constitutes the first manifestation of a nation's identity," Babingo emphasized.

In the course of their deliberations which certainly had not been short of stormy sessions, did the committee members manage to convince themselves that there could be no independence, if the citizens they had become, continued to reflect and express themselves by means of a foreign language and culture?

That notwithstanding, they agreed on the suggestion to design and launch, without any further delay, a clear language policy, capable of promoting the use of national languages. They were also of the common view that the State would need to shed off its passive attitude in that regard and rather involve itself, from the onset, in the process instead of leaving the initiative to only international and nongovernmental organizations.

The committee members recognized that the promotion of national languages required a close collaboration between several specialists and professionals: political leaders, linguists, sociologists, educationists, anthropologists, and psychologists.

Courageously, they identified four eligible languages, basing their choice on the fact that these were the four big linguistic families of the country. They also recommended, for piloting, the creation of model schools where teaching would be delivered in national languages up to the end of elementary school, according to the geographical area concerned.

The balance between French and the national language taught should begin from the second year of basic education up to the end of primary school.

The radical approach which would have meant teaching solely in national languages throughout the duration of primary school education did not meet with the approval of all the committee members.

To put an end to the opposition emanating notably from the intellectuals who clung to the advantages that the mastery of French was providing them, they were given a bone to chew on. It was decided to redesign the roles played by French and national languages. The committee members therefore envisaged conditionally tying the entry into public office to the mastery of two languages: French and a national language. This would, they thought, be the means of winning over the most reluctant members and their supporters to the learning and speaking of national languages.

The committee members left their conclave approving a plan entitled *"Manifesto for an Educational System that valorizes Cultural Heritage: Introduction of National Languages in Primary Education"*.

This important document which comprised context, rationale, and recommendations left none in doubt about the seriousness of the deliberations of the specialists.

The final plenary discussions of the Committee were mere formalities. The last argument came from the umbrella association of teachers, who threatened to embark on a strike if they were not allowed to scrutinize the plan captured in the *Manifesto* and to give their view on it. During the meetings of the National Assembly on Education, the most significant amendments such as the distinction between national languages and mother tongues were established. True to type, the teachers insisted on the need to increase their numbers and to offer a special status and incentive package to their colleagues who would teach in French and in at least one national language.

However, the principle of teaching in national languages was unanimously accepted.

At that point in time, Babingo prided himself on having overcome all obstacles.

Unfortunately, in the revised version of the Babingo Reform, the *Manifesto* underwent its first setbacks when, under pressure from the forces of inertia and conservatism, Babingo and his team were asked to submit the *Manifesto* to a Joint Ministerial Commission. There was the need to scrutinize the financial implications of a major educational and systemic reform that this revolutionary project entailed.

Predictably, the control of the fate of the *Manifesto* was totally outside the control of both Babingo, the Deputy Minister, and the Minister of Education, as it dropped in the lap of another super minister, that of Finance. Each of the eight ministerial departments threw in its two cents. The multiple amendments elicited as much well-articulated counter-proposals from Babingo. During this time, the Joint Ministerial Commission, with the material benefits due to its members for their participation at stake, continued its work. The numerous commissioners could only wish that their deliberations would never end.

After many months of back and forth, the Ministry of Finance dropped the bombshell: no provision had been made for the project in the budget of the on-going year! The possible inclusion of a budget line for the project had to be deferred till another fiscal year, while keeping an eye on the necessity to respond to the needs of priority sectors, for example agriculture. Between culture and agriculture, what should the choice be?

The *Manifesto* did not cease to shuttle back and forth from one ministry to the other for many months. There was still and always the need to put new finishing touches to it.

After it had finally been placed on the agenda of Cabinet, its assessment kept being postponed from session to session until it was put off indefinitely.

Chapter Eighteen

The labour unions of public servants declared an indefinite general strike, in solidarity with teachers and health workers. The State owed them arrears of occupational hazard allowance and responsibility allowance which it had failed to pay despite firm assurances and commitments dating back to several months. The argument of limited fiscal space, arising from the difficult prevailing economic crisis, which was advanced by the Government did not convince the civil servants.

The entire country was paralyzed because of the strike actions of the public service. The general stalemate had provoked a serious political crisis which culminated in a massive cabinet reshuffle.

In the last news broadcast on both radio and television, the post of Deputy Minister of Culture and Literacy was scrapped and subsumed under Ministry of Culture and Tourism.

Babingo learnt at his own expense that he had just been made *an ex-minister!* According to officialese, he had been deployed to another office. And yet, he was not aware of this new assignment since nobody had deigned to inform him of it beforehand.

And, later in the news, Babingo learnt that he had been appointed Head of Department of Applied Linguistics in the Faculty of Arts and Human Sciences of the only national University.

But Babingo refused to give up. Desirous of saving what he considered the work of his life, he solicited for a meeting with President Matoungoulou. He was unsuccessful.

Busy with multiple engagements, the President was not available, and particularly so as the request was coming from an ex-member of a dissolved government. The doors of the only man with the power to decide the future of the *Manifesto* seemed thus closed to Babingo for good.

In a final desperate bid, Intu Ngolo Babingo decided to create a broad-based citizens' movement that cut across political, ethnic, or religious affiliations. The citizens' movement set itself the task of awakening the consciousness of the masses, victims of the cultural and linguistic alienation facilitated by some members of the intellectual elite. It was of no use trying to make these intellectual elites *conscious of their unconsciousness!*

Babingo returned to the national university where in the end, he was assigned the ordinary position of researcher in the Department of Linguistics.

He was rather coldly welcomed by his colleagues who considered him a politician pitchforked to the University. As a result, he came up against the indifference, if not hostility, of faculty when he revealed his plans to them.

They were for the most part preoccupied with the findings of their orthodox research, some on general linguistics and sociolinguistics, others on Negro-African linguistics, and still others on ancient languages and civilizations. The introduction of national languages therefore appeared far remote from the areas of interest of these researchers, with the sole exception of Boutoulou, charged with the remit of developing a monograph on national languages.

Beyond using his new office to put finishing touches to the lexis and grammatical rules of the Téké language, Babingo also succeeded in closely associating Boutoulou with the research work that he had started earlier on the method of standardization of the Téké language. Both of them challenged themselves to formalize the use of knowledge and build a model cartography of the three major linguistic families of the country.

Chapter Nineteen

Babingo decided to no longer "disturb" politicians but to act in order to put an end to an educational system inherited from the past. He wanted to implement his plan for the creation of a truly popular and functional citizens' movement, alive to the defense of the totality of the national languages of the country. To do that, he needed to design a new approach to the question and place issues in a better people-centered perspective. There was the imperious need of convincing the rural masses of the importance of introducing their languages in the educational system.

Reading, writing, and counting for example in Lari, Bacongo, Téké, and other languages would reduce illiteracy, help these people to better organize themselves, and to value their agricultural productivity, thereby shielding them from all manner of frustrations and exploitation.

Nonetheless, how was he to win over opponents hiding behind the Constitution to demand an improbable decision from Parliament before any change? How would the minorities be convinced that their mother tongues are part of the national heritage as much as those big linguistic families which would be elevated to the status of national languages?

Tessa, who had always supported Babingo in his ambitious project, still identified with his ideals but scolded him:

"What bee's gotten into your bonnet to all of a sudden desire to create a so-called citizens' movement? Do you not know that politicians will think that you want to hide behind this name to create a political party? There is a thin line between that position and accusing you of plotting to subvert constituted authority. I therefore advise you to rather set up community activists' clubs across the length and breadth of the country."

"How would I be able to create such clubs? " Babingo asked his friend, visibly perplexed.

"Often, the political class hides behind formalities when it doesn't put forward financial arguments to avoid taking radical decisions, even if these positively impact the future of the country. It acts on the short-term, keeping only an eye on the dates for election. Taking a decision to impose two or three national languages on everyone, by basing the choice on the three major linguistic families of the country is a decision too unpopular and unwise in the opinion of politicians.

"The muted or declared reservations must be circumvented by creating a club of activists in each district, each commune, and village. Creating a club is the most innocuous approach. That would raise no suspicions from politicians."

"What could be, according to you, the role of such clubs and how will their activities be coordinated?" Babingo asked.

"You'll need to find a name both a meaningful and a striking name for the envisaged coordinating organization. Local neighborhood clubs can also be established in all our three major cities and indeed, all districts throughout the country. In addition, you'll need to sufficiently arm yourself with convincing arguments to win the support of the rural people.

"To start with, we must organize a conference on the theme: *Official Language and National Languages in the School, a Necessary Marriage.*

The success or failure of this theme with young and old will allow us to gauge the degree of interest that your initiative really generates. If, as I believe, there's a popular strong support, the creation of a coordinating organization of the activities of the clubs for the defense of national languages will be a simple formality. It's from supporters in the cities that we'll find volunteers to spread the good word to the people throughout the country."

***

The active participation in the Conference and the popular support received were so strong that Babingo had no difficulty selecting volunteers ready to crisscross the country to spread the good word.

However, the volunteers had to first be prepared, according to their departments of origin, for a relatively difficult mission that is, convincing the people of the rural communities of the fact that the mainstreaming of national languages into the curriculum would not at all be a project against the self-fulfillment of the children.

Babingo, Tessa and some others designed a series of promotional leaflets presented in the form of bilingual brochure whose content every activist had to own in order to deliver it with conviction wherever he or she went. Here is an extract:

Why introduce national languages in schools? Will the teaching of one of the national languages lower the general standard of formal education and of children's skills?

How would the literacy of adults and the uneducated youth in national languages help them in their activities? Knowing how to read, write and count in their own language or in that of one of the languages of the big linguistic families of the country, would it not help them to overcome numerous frustrations?

Would the learning and compulsory use of one of the national languages be detrimental to minority languages which also constitute an invaluable heritage of the nation?

Was it not time to demand that leaders and other politicians talk to people in the languages that they the people understand instead of "bombarding" them with speeches in language incomprehensible to the overwhelming majority?

Such was broadly the content of the pamphlet of the perfect activist.

The activists from the capital city had as directive to jointly experiment, with their colleagues in the villages and rural communities, the system of teaching in one of the identified three languages by the linguists. *Kituba*, language of the Koongo group, *Téké* and *Mbosi* were preferred by the highest number of people.

Imaginary questions in the pamphlets were transformed into affirmations that everyone wanted and identified with. Village chiefs also joined forces with the activists to participate in the literacy campaign in the major language of their locality. The young and the aged saw and appreciated the concrete benefits that accrued to them from the use of national languages.

Chapter Twenty

The reopening of schools was drawing close and already incredible and persistent rumors were reaching Babingo and his friends about the demands of the activists' clubs. From all the nooks and crannies of the country, the inhabitants were demanding, by means of petitions and other channels, the incorporation of national languages into the educational system, that is, placement on an equal footing with the official language, French.

During this time, the Minister of Education was, as expected, busy with his preparations for the reopening of school. The demands of the activists were, at best, considered a recurrent but transient and secondary phenomenon. For some die-hard supporters of bureaucracy, it was impossible to have an amendment of the Constitution with respect to the only official and working language, French. For others, the activists were only naive dreamers, nostalgic about prehistoric Africa, Africa of the Caveman. The demands of the defenders of the introduction of national languages in the educational system were besides considered inspired by a minority of Africanists hankering after recognition.

"There's no cause for alarm, Balossa the super Minister spurted, "since all parents have registered their children in school for the reopening."

The national coordination presided over by Babingo had duly submitted all the petitions coming from all activists to decision makers. Although they had conveyed the dissatisfaction of the people and their resoluteness to the people in authority, it was checkmate

everywhere. Strengthened by the demonstrations carried out by linguists on the availability
of the necessary tools for the takeoff of teaching in one of the national languages, teams
of activists in the rural areas started literacy
courses in national languages guided by the
particular language chosen for that community.

On school resumption day, Babingo was
alerted by one of the groups in the south of
the country.

"Listen, Intu Ngolo Babingo, we, from the
Mamboula group, refuse to send our children to foreign school where teaching is done
solely in a language that is not ours. We in
this community demand that henceforth and
with immediate effect, *Kituba* be integrated in
the educational system at the same level as the
so-called official language. It's not enough to
gain nominal independence; it's also necessary
to gain cultural independence."

Babingo had no time to digest this news as
he received a call that three other groups had

taken a cue from the first group. Other groups of rural and urban activists also adopted the same watchword. Soon, the totality of the nation was seized by the frenzy of school strike and a tide of discontent. Babingo had only one concern: defusing the crisis. He looked for ways of meeting the super Minister of Education in the hope of at least obtaining a favourable response, or a mere assurance. He waited all day, in vain.

The following day, schools remained without students. Then began the hounding of the activists everywhere across the length and breadth of the country.

Leaders of the groups and the national coordinator were to respond to the serious accusation levelled against them as agitators. Babingo was summoned by Balossa, the super Minister of Education who had not deigned to respond to his request for a meeting.

"Babingo, we did not send you to the Department of Linguistics of the national University to create problems for the country. You know that your crazy obsession to introduce at all cost what you call national languages in the curriculum is, in the actual context, anything but reasonable. The country is facing an unprecedented economic crisis. Our government, composed of technocrats in the majority, has as mission the rectification of the socio-economic malaise of the country. You are sufficiently educated to know that there are priorities.

"I am asking you to immediately put a stop to the strike in the schools, otherwise you and your followers should be prepared not just for trials of an administrative nature but also for terrible legal proceedings."

"Balossa my dear colleague and Honourable Minister, I observe that we no longer relate to each other on first-name terms, because in your opinion, I am already liable to trial, an outlaw.

"I must confess that I know nothing about the strike order given by the groups of activists across the country.

"For a long time, the masses have been expecting the order from the people at the top, from those who know everything, do everything on behalf of those who elected them and whom the people in authority are supposed to represent. It seems this time is over and that those below want to take their destiny into their own hands.

"Naturally, my friends and I have made the masses aware of the fact that their means of expression, and consequently their way of understanding the world, have eluded them for too long. Do I need to repeat that learning in a language that is foreign to you contributes to plunging you into permanent alienation? I am convinced of it and I realize that our compatriots accept less and less to continue to experience this frustration.

"The response to the expectations of our compatriots is in your hands."

"No, my dear Intu Ngolo Babingo, I know that one word from you will be enough to put a stop to this school strike. You've been a member of the government; therefore, you know perfectly well that we can't agree to a populist demand coming from the street. The President of the Republic, the Head of Government, His Excellency Matoungoulou Dieudonné, won't agree that schools be boycotted for two days just because certain individuals demand that, with a magic wand, national languages are incorporated into the curriculum."

Babingo, who had understood the reasons for the friendly tone his former colleague wanted to adopt, continued to address him in a formal tone.

"Honorable Minister, contrary to what you think, it is not about certain individuals but about a general protest which mobilizes practically all the layers of the society. If I were in your shoes, I would not trivialize such a protest involving both from cities and villages. For, if the people in the cities are known for being critical of the government, our fellow citizens in the rural areas do not have the interest to revolt at the drop of a hat."

"Babingo, it's always easy to be on the side of insurgents when one isn't in power, when one no longer has national responsibilities. For the second time, I'm asking you to intervene to end this strike. The Head of State will be informed of our discussion. Should I tell him that you'll make an effort or that on the contrary, you've refused to be reasonable?"

"Tell the Head of State to ask one of his close associates to intervene to calm tempers down. And if it is he himself who addresses the activists to reassure them by making a commitment on what his government is ready to do to satisfy these people who are hungry for authenticity, it would be better still."

Super Minister Balossa took Babingo's response to mean a refusal to cooperate. In the morning of the third day of the school strike, at six o'clock a group of heavily armed men showed up uninvited in front of the residence of Babingo and his partner.

An officer knocked at the door with force howling: "Open, open!" Gripped with fear, Babingo half-opened the door which was then violently thrown open by one of the visitors.

"Are you Intu Ngolo Babingo?"

"Yes, responded the latter. "For what reason do you come to my house this early?"

"You have been harbouring a foreigner who entered the country illegally. We must take both of you to the police so that you can account for your actions."

"Ingrid is my partner. She is therefore under my protection. She entered the country with a visa; it is true that it has expired."

"You will explain all that to the officer when we arrive at the police office."

Babingo and Ingrid, who complied with the police order, boarded a small van, surrounded by four men. Once in the office of the inspector in charge of the interrogation, they had to state their identities and then undergo a series of cross-examinations.

Ingrid Jöndöttir had to explain how she entered the country and why she was continuing to stay there with a visiting visa whose validity had expired a long time ago. Why had she not presented herself to the immigration department for a possible extension of this visa? What did she go to look for at Odiba village?

Ingrid was able to respond calmly to the questions. But her explanations and above all her justifications appeared unusual in the eyes of her interlocutor. Moreover, her militancy on the side of the activists was deemed suspicious.

But, while she was responding to the interrogations, she realized that the police officer had on his two cheeks beautiful scarifications which showed that he belonged to the Téké ethnic group. As if to make her story better understood, she started to relate, in perfect Téké language, the details of her coming to the country and of her stay in Odiba, Mama

Mamatouka's village. Puzzled by the foreigner's mastery of his mother tongue, the police officer was divided between his sympathy for her and his sense of discipline towards a person liable to trial.

The police officer continued to record Ingrid's story in French. He felt relieved when he was able to end the recording of the foreigner's statement. He turned to Babingo.

"Why have you harboured and kept in your house a foreigner with an irregular status?"

"As I already explained to your colleague this morning, Ingrid is my partner. She has just narrated to you in detail the circumstances of her presence in our country."

"What proves that you are a regular couple? Nothing. You are not married. Therefore, no legal connection.

"Besides, she has an irregular status. In her case, we should keep her under watch here until the day of her deportation. It is not ruled out that you also will be tried for complicity of fraud for having kept a foreigner in your house, and in a clandestine manner at that. However, in this special case, Madam Ingrid Jöndöttir will not be kept in custody. She has forty-eight hours to leave the country. As for you, even if you are freed today, you should expect the judge asking you for explanations one of these days."

Although Babingo protested, ran around to convince various officials about Ingrid's honesty and his right to have a partner of his choice, nothing worked. All doors had been closed to him. The airport in the capital city was jam-packed with men and women, young and old, wearing around their necks a yellow nylon scarf which set the activists apart from the other people around. They were there to show their solidarity to Ingrid who was being compelled to leave the country.

All the delegates of the groups from the various localities were present, some with flowers, some with a typical art work in their hands, to signify their sympathy more for Ingrid as a valiant activist than as Babingo's partner. Observers would easily have believed that they were witnessing a high ranking personality's departure on a journey, if the faces of the activists were not so inscrutable, telltale signs of sadness and pent-up anger.

But the law had to take its course and Ingrid had to return by air to her native Iceland. Far from undermining their morale, the measure which hit Babingo through his partner, rather strengthened the resolve of the activists.

Chapter Twenty-One

On the fourth day of the strike, no dialogue had yet begun between the activists and the government. On the contrary, diverse strategies had been set in motion to weaken the protest. The leaders of the groups had to hide to avoid being arrested. Tessa had the greatest fright of her life when a vehicle of the Ministry of the Interior stopped in front of her residence this Sunday morning. Two police officers in civilian clothes, with intimidating looks, stepped out of the vehicle after assuring themselves that no curious onlooker was monitoring their movements.

At first, Tessa thought that the visitors had come to look for her husband on a matter concerning his labour union protest, as there was general unrest at that time.

"Good day, are you Madam Tessa?"

"Yes, I am."

"We've the order to escort you to the Minister of the Interior who desires to meet with you personally."

"To what do I deserve this honour of invitation from Minister Pindi?"

"We aren't in a position to tell you; our duty is to ask you to stop everything you're doing and follow us."

Tessa had the presence of mind to inform Okima Maurice, her husband, who had left home very early to support the strike of the teaching personnel which had started two days earlier. Outside, a handful of neighbours and onlookers had surrounded the official vehicle with the aim of preventing it from taking off in case Tessa was under arrest. But she reassured everybody, claiming that it was for a meeting which she herself had requested several months earlier. The car pulled away without let or hindrance toward the asphalted street that led to the classy neighbourhoods where the Ministry of the Interior was sited.

At the gate of this outrageously secured edifice, the vehicle had to stop to undergo a thorough search conducted by two soldiers who, after going round it, looked hard at the occupants to reassure themselves that the driver was indeed the one they knew and that he was free to move as he liked.

In the huge courtyard of the Ministry, a group of armed soldiers was positioned at the main entrance of the building and the Minister's office. One of the officers escorting Tessa led her into the office of the personal secretary where she received an excessively formal and warm welcome. After a military salute to the minister, the .officer immediately left.

The Minister of the Interior, Honourable Pindi, stood up to welcome Tessa. He started by greeting her in Kituba, perhaps as a way of showing her that he was not against the introduction of national languages, but probably to remind her that they were both members of the same ethnic group. This show of charm did not seem to fool Tessa who was rather on her guard. Still in Kituba and with gestures, the Minister attacked Tessa.

"While we're battling to confront the numerous socio-economic problems that the country is bedevilled with, your friends and you have chosen to incite the masses over the issue of national languages. May I remind you that this government is not indifferent to it, but it has other priorities relating to the recruitment of teachers, their training and their remunerations, the reorientation of our policy in order to guarantee food self-sufficiency in the medium term. Numerous commitments are waiting to be fulfilled and you, you find nothing else to do than to create chaos across the country under the pretext of wanting to introduce national languages in our educational system.

"I count on you to bring this unreasonable strike to an end. Let the children go to school, for their individual future and that of the entire country depend on it."

"No," replied Tessa. "The education that is being provided today is rather dehumanizing; it's far from guaranteeing the future of our children. Please remember that one only truly learns when one understands. Now, in their great majority, children living in the rural areas must make extraordinary efforts to acquire knowledge in a language which is not theirs. It isn't surprising that it's in this environment that one records most failures and school dropouts.

"Development must be endogenous, founded on the aspirations and genuine needs of the masses. It isn't by imposing an educational system inherited from the colonial era that you're going to ensure the development of the country. Food security will come from the improvement of agricultural practices, from a genuine agricultural reform, from farmers better educated in their languages and motivated because aware that they can ultimately and always live decently on their work."

Honorable Pindi jumped up agitated and finally rose from his massif wooden armchair which probably was made from the best wood species of the country. He went near Tessa and sat on a chair next to her. He continued his plea softly, so softly that it seemed he was whispering a secret.

"Sister, I advise you to stop following the handful of intellectuals yearning for a revolution. Their protest is destined for failure, because the President won't ever accept that children are prevented from going to school for a long time. When things are back in order, he envisages carrying out a reshuffling of the government. It isn't unlikely that he'll call around him active personalities like you to head the

Department of Social Affairs. It's, in a way, an indiscretion on my part that I'm giving you this privileged information which I want you to keep to yourself. If, for your part, you make an effort to bring an end to the ardour of the group of activists by making a simple statement on the necessity to stop the strike and to resort to negotiations, the Head of State will reward you for that."

Tessa took the Minister's proposal for an insult. Because he was asking her to manipulate her colleagues in the groups by suggesting abandonment of the only arm which the activists possessed to bring the authorities to cease from prevaricating on the question of national languages.

"I'm not in a position to dictate to the leaders of the groups the means of arriving at their ends," Tessa said, very annoyed by the politician's proposal.

"You seem not to understand that the protest came from the masses themselves who have become conscious of the alienation which for them was the fact that they think in a language that isn't theirs. Besides, as you know, majority of our fellow citizens don't understand anything from the speeches that are incessantly thrown at them by duty bearers.

"Therefore, avoid reversing the course of events by asking activists to stop their strike as a condition for negotiations. They're waiting for concrete actions, in the short run, if not immediately."

Pindi threw a fit of anger, causing the feet of the chair he was occupying close to Tessa to be grated. He went to sit before his ministerial table on top of which the portrait of a good-natured President Matoungoulou sat majestically.

"You can't understand, since you know nothing at all about the ordeals of power. I hope you won't regret your obstinacy, sooner or later."

Tessa's scarcely veiled refusal to collaborate completely displeased Minister Pindi who, as a result, parted company with his recalcitrant interlocutor unceremoniously. Tessa related the details of the story of her meeting with the politician to Babingo and other leaders of the groups of activists. The daring proposals of Minister Pindi were considered an admission of weakness, proof of governmental incapacity to take a bold decision on the country's future.

Chapter Twenty-Two

On the fifth day of the strike, the militants displayed as much firmness as they had done at the beginning of the protest. Very quickly, the international press picked up the details of the protests of the people who were claiming for themselves and for their offspring the right to be educated in their own language. A people who wanted to finally safeguard their identity in order to better open up to the world.

That day, Tessa was surprised to receive a telephone call from one of her former classmates who had left the country for North America. Sana, who had studied journalism in Canada, arrived in the country to interview

Tessa to learn more about the root causes of the school strike and the course it was taking. As a competent special correspondent, Sana wasted no time sending her scoop to her press agency. The news spread like wild fire. All overseas media houses picked up Sana's report. Unfavourable commentaries made the headlines to condemn this country where authorities remained impervious to the legitimate demands of its people.

The sole Canadian television channel at the time prepared a report on the spot, filmed and broadcast across the world images of hundreds of empty schools. That was more than what the local authorities could take but nothing could stop the flow of information and commentaries on the incapability of the authorities of this country to take decisions.

All was topsy-turvy when President Matoungoulou Dieudonné summoned his ministers to an extraordinary meeting.

"It is truly deplorable that I should always intervene on your behalf and in every issue," thundered the all-powerful Head of State.

"It has been more than five days that the country has been experiencing very disturbing moments of unrest, unique in its history. Schools are closed because of a strike and our Minister of Health, Works and Education, Youth and Sports wait for the solution to come from the President.

"The Minister of the Interior is doing nothing to stop the protests which have spread into the cities and towns, and worse, into the hinterland. The district commissioners who are supposed to represent the executive arm in the various communities have found no means of mobilizing majority of the local chiefs to support the government. On the contrary, most of them have been won over to the cause of the activists.

"The whole country is paralyzed. And we have become the laughing stock of the world

press. It seems we are incapable of responding to the aspirations of a people who are
demanding for their identity by insisting on the
introduction of national languages in the educational system.

"At the time when we are trying to convince
our eternal partners of the necessity to support
us in the implementation of our development
programme, these strikes could not have come
at the worse time. For people are watching and
none would come to invest in a country that is
experiencing social upheavals."

President Matoungoulou was speaking like
that, but, deep inside him, he knew that no
minister was capable of suggesting a solution
out of the crisis. Every initiative should come
from him and from him alone.

The President looked round in rage in the
direction of the ministers seated around the
vast meeting table, focusing his attention on the
heads of the two ministries in question. And
although a brother-in-law, the man in charge

of Internal Affairs mournfully seemed to be kissing good-bye to the hope he had earlier nourished of seeing his ministry elevated to the status of Ministry of State.

One could almost hear a pin drop, with the august meeting room engulfed in silence, that Wednesday.

Still holding the floor, Matoungoulou concluded, peremptorily:

"I am asking the heads of the Ministries of Education and Interior to present to me, forthwith and within twenty-four hours, a bill to be submitted to Parliament on the introduction of the three languages already identified by the specialists. It will be necessary to mobilize all resources, human and financial, in order that the programme does not suffer any delay.

"I will meet the Speaker of Parliament[9] to request him to proceed in such manner that the bill be debated and approved under a certificate

9   The counterpart of this personality in Francophone African
    countries is often called the "President of the National Assembly"
    (Président (e) de l'Assemblée nationale) or "President of Parlia-
    ment" ("Président(e) du Parlement."

of emergency. For, all efforts must be deployed for the reform to come into effect by the next reopening of schools.

Parliament met in an emergency session and unanimously passed the Law incorporating three national languages into the educational system with effect from the following academic year.

All obstacles were ironed out. Linguists were mobilized for the fine-tuning of the manuals whose broad framework had already been outlined. So also were logistics and procurement officials called upon to ensure the seamless transportation of required materials throughout the length and breadth of the nation. Specialist teachers were reoriented and empowered to use both French and one of the chosen languages, to share with learners, their knowledge of diverse subjects.

That is how in Intu Ngolo Babingo's country, Téké and two other vernaculars were promoted to the rank of national languages to be taught as compulsory subjects right from the very first year of school.

Glossary of Names

Alagablettur:	Towns built in the rocks and inhabited by Huldufolks.
Balossa:	Super minister, in charge of Health, Works, Education, Youth and Sports.
David Dupont:	Headmaster of Sacred Heart College in Bagnères-de-Bigorres, France.
Dieudonné Matoungoulou:	New Head of State.
Galin Doite:	Paul Makouta's friend.
Huldufolk:	Invisible people in Iceland mythology.
Ingrid Jöndöttir	Alex Babingo's Icelandic friend who became his partner.
Intu Ngolo:	"Strong head," replaced Babingo's first name, following his rejection of Alex.
Jön Einarson:	Ingrid's father.
Kamanga:	Deposed Head of State.
Kieli Makouta:	Babingo's aunt.
Kassissi and Massissi:	Two sisters who are Babingo's cousins.
Madeleine Mamakouta:	Babingo's mother.
Mananga and Dibomba:	The two army officers, sympathizers of the insurgents who deposed Kamanga.

Makolondinga:	Representative of the Imano lineage, Mamakouta's ethnic group.
mwana yu kikimayô :	A child of wonder; Kikimayô is the first name given to this child born from a first and only love affair.
Nga Babatolé:	The great diviner of Odiba village.
Nga Npandu:	Hunter-healer who initiated Babingo into the secret of traditional medicine.
Nkuna:	Local name for the city of Brazzaville.
Odiba:	Mamakouta's home village.
Okima Maurice:	Trade Unionist and Tessa's husband.
Paul Makouta:	Babingo's father.
Pindi:	Minister of Interior.
Sana:	Journalist, from Canada, she interviewed Tessa, her friend.
Simi (line that speaks)	Telephone in Icelandic language.
Tessa:	Babingo's childhood friend.
Vegabref (road document)	Passport in Icelandic language.

Printed in the United States
by Baker & Taylor Publisher Services